D0948434

THE
JONAH
WATCH

THE
JONAH
WATCH

*A True-life Ghost Story
in the Form of a Novel*

by JACK CADY

ARBOR HOUSE
New York

FOR CAROL, A FELLOW HISTORIAN

So Jonah Arose, and Went Unto Nineveh,
According to the Word of the Lord.

—Jonah 3:3

Author's note:

~~~~~~

THIS TALE remembers the cutters *Yankton* and *Legare*, and the men who sailed them. Experienced seamen who recall the early 1950s, which is the setting for this story, will see that the Coast Guard cutter *Adrian* is a conglomerate of the 125-foot and 110-foot classes.

As to the spectral, other-worldly nature of what follows: I never saw a Coast Guard log doctored, but I have seen events that were deliberately omitted. Each incident in this story actually occurred in one form or another. The ghost of Jensen (a fictional name) appeared climbing the ladder to the bridge of a neighboring cutter on more than one occasion. The incident of the *Hester C.* (another fictional name) is a matter of record, although the spectral manifestation that accompanied it is not. I have no explanation for these events, nor seek any. They happened. I witnessed them while in a state of sobriety when I am firmly convinced I was not crazy.

All other events are a matter of official record, whether they be six downed airmen, or a terrible case of epilepsy. In the cause of fiction it has been necessary to change the tactical disposition of cutters, while names of vessels towed are entirely fictional. However, the names are common to that coast. Here and there they may accidentally match the name of a real vessel.

Like the ship, the crew is a conglomerate of characteristics observed among hundreds of seamen. The exceptions are Masters and Racca. No doubt there are plenty of men on that coast who have no courage, but this writer has met only one. His name was quite a common name, and he was old and tired and failing in the business of fishing. In his younger days, it was said of him that he had been brave.

Last, this book is an exercise in total recall. It took a year to write, but the only research material needed was a chart of the coast. In a way the book took more than a year. I first tried it in '61, then in '69, then in '73, and finally wrote it in 1980. I left the Coast Guard in '56. It took twenty-four years to gather enough skill and objectivity to tell the story. My admiration for those unsung men who save life at sea was so great that sentiment blocked the earlier attempts.

THE
JONAH
WATCH

I

~~~~~~

ON THOSE far northern shores where the wind
sets north-northeast, and where remote lighthouses are haunted
by dark tales of men flung upright from the surf—as if the dead
rose through spray like pathetic divines—the summer slides in
on the memory of ice. Sunlight polishes the luminous green of
the outer islands. Old men unprop their feet from crackling
wood stoves. They stop their winter yarning; stretch, turn
weathered faces to the sun. Brick streets glisten with melt from
high-piled banks and stockades and walls of snow. Young men
blink fantastically in the sun. Their downeast, high-bowed
vessels no longer plunge doubled up on the moorings. The
young men hunger and begin to laugh. They seem strangely
unamazed to be alive.

The summer shuffle begins. There is a last-minute rearrange-
ment of crews aboard the trawlers. Nets repaired during
winter and deemed "twill do" seem old and fragile in the sun.
The ships' chandlers enjoy a surge of business, dealing almost
lustily in the perfume of manila, of tarred marlin, of enameled

boxes of electronics designed to aid in the taking of fish. To the east the swells bat down and the North Atlantic settles promissory toward the tranquillity of summer. On the white ships, arc welders sputter against winter damage. Here and there a new face appears, a new set of hands, a new body to be groomed and trained and then thrown against the inevitability of September.

Ernie Brace came aboard on a day that surrounded the cutter *Adrian* with the over-flooding certainty of sunlight. The tide was full and the gangway taut, for the tidal fall in those waters is great. When the tide was at half, the gangway pointed straight across from ship to pier. It gave rattles like the clank of pans being beaten by chains. At full tide the gangway pinged like a drumhead telegraphing the uncertainty of Brace's steps. He moved like any other seaman deuce sprung high-schooled and timid from the fields and small towns of Indiana or Kansas. His fresh seabag was glazed white in the sun. It hung stiff over a narrow shoulder that leaned with its weight. Brace's slender body was clad in issue blues, like a brushed and newly blocked sack from which popped his unremarkable-appearing, brown-haired head—a head, some supposed, that was stuffed with young arrogance which the man would not lose until he had survived some heavy weather.

He was new to the ship, but he represented nothing new. They come and go, these young ones, like confused cherubs or corn-fed angels ashore in Rome. Plunking untraveled seabags to the quarterdeck, they cause small ripples as they enter the community of the ship, only to soon leave with no trace of a wake. They go to service schools or by draft to weather cutters. They are great requesters of transfers—or were.

Yet, it does not seem long ago. We were all rougher then, as we are certainly smoother now. Those who are not sand-papered flat.

The sea is the same, and the brawling northeastern ports remain. The narrow white Coast Guard ships churn white froth as they appear and disappear like phantoms into shrouds of mist. These new ones are bright with bold red stripes on their bows and with commission pennants snapping from stubby masts; yet, they hold a hint of other ships. They tell a subdued vision of converted subchaser hulls made awkward by high boxlike deckhouses. Short fantails disappear into a winter fog of memory, but yes—the sea is the same. Mist and the sparkle of sun turned dull on polished bronze, and always, finally, the ice fog and ash-gray light of winter. What seems a tale of the wind is really a tale of ice and the mist.

Brace blinked in that sun and looked at his first assignment. Confused. His mouth was not naturally large and now it was tight. His dark eyes were more fearful than timid. It must have seemed to him that he had been sent to the very belly of chaos.

Beneath his hand a rail twisted away; the round, solid steel grotesquely bent like half a question. Before his eyes, a second rail twisted downward from the boat deck. Foundations, where gear lockers once stood, looked like an erect tumble of steel shrubbery, while the lockers themselves, as Brace would discover, were taking a swim off Georges Bank. Cutter *Adrian* was poxed with spots of red lead over newly cleaned steel. The house was streaked with rusty slashes of new welds that bled toward the deck. On the boat deck beside twisted and empty davits two seamen stopped their work, nudged each other, laughed; winked like a couple engaged in an extravagant romance. They waited for chief bosun Dane to appear, stubby legged and bawling. On the fantail the yeoman, Howard, nursed a light hangover and checked a requisition of stores. He bit at the end of a yellow pencil and rubbed his aching, dark-haired head. Through the open midship hatch sounded the curse of an engineman and the rattle of chain falls. The radio made desultory pops from the bridge. The steward Amon scampered aft . . . stopped; his olive Hawaiian face managed to look bland and incredulous at the same time.

"New man?"

"Brace. Where should I go?"

"I make your acquaintance Brace—make it later," and Amon chugged toward the after hatch bearing news.

Coils of towline hung like wheat-colored festoons along the undamaged areas of rail. The 20-mm guns were shrouded in canvas. They pointed skyward like small, clothed steeples. Brace looked forward, looked aft, moved an indecisive step. The 125-foot length of *Adrian* seemed a tattered and inchoate jumble. He eased his unspotted seabag onto a small patch of tar, and the cook, Lamp, having received the news of a new mouth and stomach, bumped through the after hatch in time to see bosun Dane appear like a moving gargoyle from forward.

Men stopped work. Waited. Whispered and chuckled. On the boat deck, one of the seamen bounced on his heels like an ape, rolled his eyes to heaven, gurgled a poor imitation of a death rattle. Brace stood confused and unsuspecting. Dane approached as surely as the tide.

He was toadlike with rheumatism, Dane, and he stood in that crew like a minor god when the sun shone, like Jehovah, Itself, during gale. In this crucial matter of saving life and property at sea, it was known that when the wind blew black from the northeast, Dane's rheumatism went before it. In the winter just past, a frozen and nearly whipped deck gang had watched Dane balance on a pitching rail and put a heaving line accurately into the teeth of a forty-knot blow. He was hated by some, respected by all, and he was secretly loved—as those who are unreligious may still think kindly of the Madonna.

Water slapped the pier. Gulls squawked. Brace reported.

"Another tailwagger." Dane reached for the thin service record which was as stiff and new between its covers as Brace's seabag. Dane fanned himself with the record and puffed. He stood erect for a moment, then slumped back to the demands of rheumatism. He was a blockish sort. A troll. Short and heavy with thin lips, thick forearms, thick waist. He sniffed as if he sensed the presence of a garbage scow. He seemed to be listening to the gulls and the silence about the decks.

"Where you from, puppy?"

Brace admitted that he hailed from southern Illinois. Timid. Tremulous. A low voice from a boy who seemed unsure whether he was under attack. Wonderment crossed his smooth face. He was pained like a newsboy who is refused payment because his journal carries wrong-headed editorials.

Dane gazed with scorn. He managed to say with his manner that he had always expected somewhat more of southern Illinois. The broad, thin-lipped toad mouth was flat with disapproval. His hunched shoulders flexed. Threatening. One hand held the service record, the other flicked horny-handed to make dents in the new covers. His thick shoulders hunched and his hands seemed scarcely restrained from tearing Brace to fragments. On the boat deck a man sniggered.

Brace stepped backward, bumped the gangway with his foot, stumbled.

"Stand," Dane told him. "Stay . . . sit . . . roll over . . . play dead."

"Sir?"

"Jump through hoops . . . waggle your butt . . . say sir to officers but not to your betters . . . slather . . . chase your tail 'til you rupture . . . and shed those raggedy blues and get into dungarees."

Brace moved to pick up his seabag.

"Stand. Did I say pick that up—no—I-did-not-say-pick-that-up . . . ," and the harangue began. Did Brace have a mother? Was she proud? Why? A father? How could Brace be sure? A woman? Mona? What kind of a cornfield name was Mona? Dane warmed to his task and Brace, slow to understand, became monosyllabic and shocked.

No doubt it was the sun. The sun warmed Dane's rheumatism, and he rose joyfully to intimidation that appalled all of his previous efforts in that line. He swarmed over Brace. his words were as hot as fire in a cargo of raw sulphur. This god-blessed blankety son of a plowshare and a mule . . . his voice rose, ran the scale of sound and pitch and volume. His face became red and apoplectic. Across the pier, the crew on the cutter *Abner* stopped work and listened and whooped to encourage his raving. Dane fumed, fizzled, spat, walked heavenward through curses, while Brace first became red with anger and then redder with shame as the whoops from *Abner* centered on him like a spotlight. Dane moved easily through a cloud of metaphor and returned to the basics of Brace's high school locker room. Brace turned from fear and anger to fury. His face was white.

It was the result Dane wanted. It made him pleased. He stopped midsentence, looked at the pale, tense face and trembling hands that were not able to stay unclenched. Brace was within two seconds of forgetting the consequences of attempting murder. Dane smiled, and it was a smile like a grandfather bequeathing his gold watch to an ambitious posterity.

"You pass," Dane said. "And welcome aboard."

He turned from Brace to display the back of his neck as he bent forward to rub his knee. He hollered for Glass, seaman, and Glass tumbled down the ladder from the bridge in a panting, red-faced, hysteric scramble; as if doom had just cracked and he had a few things to attend to before the end of the world. From the boat deck came the sound of someone choking with laughter, while another man beat fists helplessly against a rolled canvas in an agony of entertainment. Glass skidded to a stop, wild-eyed, saw that the play was ended and resumed his composure. Glass was a tall, teacherly-looking Jew from the Boston slums who read detective stories and dreamed of being a professional criminal.

"It's the way we do it here," Glass said to Brace. "You can get used to almost anything," and he led the trembling Brace below decks like a nurse leading a patient who suffers from tottering old age.

18

II

‹‹‹‹‹‹‹‹‹‹‹‹‹‹‹‹‹‹‹‹‹‹‹‹‹‹‹‹‹‹‹‹‹‹‹‹‹

"BOYS, BOYS . . . . " In later years, when he ran the mess at the South Portland Base, the cook, Reeser Lamp, would claim that he was the first man to see Brace come aboard; and he would believe it. Lamp claimed the credit as he would claim every other minor miracle during those years when he cooked aboard the cutter *Adrian.*

Lamp was a man with a propensity for miracles. On the most tedious day, he would still feel charged to understand every opaque reasoning of divinity. Nothing happened that was without meaning—if only a body could figure the meaning—and Reeser Lamp was the man with the answers. He would have made an annoying preacher or a successful spiritualist. After a lifetime spent musing on the fortunate aspects of his birth, he has now had a chance to test the final miracle. He was a good cook.

In Lamp's memory, Brace arrived on a day loaded with mixed portents. The summer with its clear and unoppressive light made the Gulf of Maine a sort of giant pond where yachtsmen flourished and lobstermen went about with their usual grumbles. Trawlers bearing the names of saints and wives and other martyrs churned beside Portland Head and the lightship. Their business was cod and their office was Georges Bank. From the moorings in South Portland it was possible to distinguish several of the thousands of islands on that rocky coast. The buoy yard smelled of barnacles and kelp and red lead: the nun buoys lay in red and black rows like components of artillery, and the lighted bells and whistles lay on tubby, slanted bases, immobile and silent like abandoned buildings. It was an easy day, and summer is a routine time for cutters assigned to search and rescue. *Adrian* and its twin, *Abner*, were moored at the pier like tired laborers slumbering.

Still, in Lamp's imagination (packed as it was with as many signs and symbols as a flag locker), there was something peculiar about the appearance of Ernie Brace on an easy day in sunlight. In those later years, cooking at the Base, Lamp would interrupt his interminable reminiscence of a tour of duty in the Far East to draw one more moral from the advent of Brace.

"Boys," he would say, "Boys, boys . . . . ," and shake his red-blond-haired head that was small above his great belly and heavy shanks. "Be double-dog-damn if I knew what I was feeling. Only somehow the luck was backward." A tawny, lionlike head; but small, like a cat's head placed over the girth of an aging rhinoceros.

A new voice would always ask the same question, and there were always plenty of new voices. The mess at that base was casual with transient sailors, ambulatories from the Marine hospital, and visitors attached to the First District offices.

"Did you know he was a Jonah, cook?"

"The luck had been bad but it was turnin'. That was that bad winter . . . . " Lamp would pause, shake the small, leonine head slowly and with genuine sorrow. *Adrian* had lost a man that winter. Cecil Jensen, an engineman, at sea and the body un-recovered. Lost with the fishing vessel *Louise*.

"Maybe it was somebody else, cook. You already were a-tough'n it."

"Backward. Not good, not bad, just backward. I be double-dog-damn if I knew what I was feeling."

By then Lamp had trouble with his legs. He did not move with the lumbering, seagoing accuracy of former days when he would prop himself against the face of the oven, or the hot bulkhead by the stove. *Adrian* was a tough sea boat, but it was a masterpiece neither of comfort nor design. It had been battered too often, was stretched toward age like fraying cable. It was reengined after each war. The original blueprints, mute be-neath stacks of outdated charts in the lower drawer of the chartbox, called for auxiliary sail.

"Did the luck change right away?"

"It didn't work that way, boys."

"I don't believe in Jonahs, cook. I don't hardly believe in admirals."

"I believe in broken legs." (This from a man wearing a cast.)

"Me, I believe in women."

"Sure now, and I believe in payday."

Cooks generally talk too much, and it is their fate to be razzed and raspberried. On these occasions Lamp would re-treat to his galley where it is said that he prayed for the souls of degenerate sailors. . . .

"Mother Lamp," seaman Glass explained to apprentice seaman Brace, as Brace unpacked the stiff, new seabag. "Howard—he's the yeoman—Howard gave him that name and it stuck." Glass turned as the small sunlight that penetrated to the crew's compartment was blocked by a silhouette. "That's Howard."

Yeoman Howard, hangover intact, was approaching with Brace's watchkeeping assignment.

"I want a transfer," Brace muttered into the mouth of the seabag. His voice was soft and still trembling from the attack by Dane. "Everybody said that it was different when you got a ship."

"Me, too," Glass said. "I want a transfer. To that *Adam* cutter in L.A. Champagne. Movie stars."

Brace rummaged deep in the bag, found a framed photograph of a young woman, looked at Glass and Howard. He dropped the photograph back into the bag.

"He's in our section," Howard told Glass.

"That gets me off the four-to-eight," Glass said. "You're a true shipmate, chum."

Brace stood looking about the shadowed interior of the crew's compartment. The odor of polished wax nearly obscured the smell of work clothes in need of washing. Bunks tiered three-deep ran the portside length of the compartment; layers of canvas, cotton and wool, pressing so close that the intimacy of other feet and butts, of sweat and beer farts and snores, was a flat statement. Brace shivered and unrolled bedding. He wrinkled his rather long but nondescript nose that was as unpimpled, unlined, and bland as his forehead.

"Seamen bunk forward," Howard told him. "You get a better ride."

"Take an upper," Glass said kindly. "Don't hardly anybody ever vomit, but why take chances?" He turned to Howard. "You was seen last night with a very evil lady."

"Is he always that way?" Brace stood holding new blankets draped over one arm. He seemed for an instant very close to tears.

"She's shy," said Howard. "Like me."

"Me, too," Glass said. "I'm shy. I got a fine mind, but it always takes ten seconds . . . . "

"Because if he is," Brace said, "then this is a zoo."

"We were just talkin' about that," Glass told him.

"This is the cutter *Adrian*," Howard said. "The captain is

Phil Levere, mustang. The chief bosun is Roy Dane. You are apprentice seaman Brace."

"He means that the old man must be slipping," Glass explained. "The District almost always sends us seamen."

"Do what you can with him," Howard told Glass. He turned away.

"A zoo . . . an absolute zoo . . . "

"Terrible man," Glass was saying as Howard disappeared up the ladder. "No consideration of us working class. Get squared away and I'll take you on a tour . . . . "

If the ship was not a masterpiece of design, the same could not be said of the crew, although when Brace joined, he would find a crew that had indeed been tough'n it. Mother Lamp had good reason to cluck and worry.

After a winter of continued shock, the crew walked through the sunlight like invalids given new hope. The memory of the drowned Cecil Jensen was strong. On the messdeck men still avoided sitting in what had been Jensen's customary place. In the engine room, his handwritten watch-standing orders maintained his presence. An engineman first class with six years aboard a vessel is not easily erased.

The crew went ashore like men with storm warnings still flying in their souls. Their hair was freshly shorn, but their heads were not light; as though the thick ruff of fur grown for a downeast winter still bowed them trembling into their foul-weather gear.

Good men. As strong and certain as the heavy-shanked and moral-headed Lamp. They appear in groups of two or three, or singly with a face poked into the mask of an antique and rickety radar, like a submariner before a periscope as *Adrian* staggers beneath blows that bring green water crashing to the bridge. They stand solid on the heaving fantail or lean against the shock of the sea, grasping with numb fingers as breaking water washes the deck to push them like arrows about to be twanged from the lifelines. Their eyebrows and watch caps glisten with ice. Like spectres they appear in the low moan of dying winds, and they amble the decks and shout and laugh. A North Atlantic mosaic of winter. A perpetual rattle of coffee mugs in the galley, the blown, delicate curve of carefully rigged lines, and the six-inch towing hawser sagging astern and shaking water from its tons, to appear three hundred yards away snugged to the bows of a distressed vessel.

Simple men and true. No better than their predecessors; no better than their successors, perhaps. A sailor takes what he finds and learns to make it work—and, of course, a red stripe on your bow does not sail the ship . . . .

When you are young, as Brace was young, the day can arrive exalted like the cadenced thunder of Kipling on his red ladder of dawn—or the dawn can mutter across the earth in an orange mist of confusion. The way you experience dawn may depend on something as simple as whether you catch the midwatch or the four-to-eight.

Dawn comes early in Maine summers. While your crew lies sleeping, you stand watch in exhilarating solitude. Dreaming—as we old men recall—of romance and the love of distant friends. The 25-amp radio crackles indifferently on the watch frequency of 2670, the globed nightlights are red and shadow-casting through the dark ship, and the harbor is a placid canvas carrying a tracery of light, a network, a web, the silent and lighted waterfront of cities. As the dawn arrives, the duty engineman appears on the main deck, stretches, gaps, yawns and sniffs the salt- and petroleum-smelling air. He scratches, as if the boredom of a cold-iron watch was palpable in his armpit and could be rubbed away. Gulls slide by in the darkness. Water pops and slushes between the hull and the pier. Across the harbor sound yells of stevedores coming to work, and distantly, the putting of a small boat carrying stores bound for a Greek or Panamanian ship swinging in quarantine. There is a rattle of pans from the galley as Lamp bustles about with thick whispers and exhortations to the Hawaiian steward Amon, who

24

is still sleepy-eyed, who will be brewing the cup of tea that gives him strength to load the huge coffee urn. With the movement of your fellows the confusion returns.

"... B–race ... "

"Get crackin'."

Dane, knowing on the brute level of the sea that there is desperately much to learn and that summer is short, pressed Brace to the limit. He cursed, scorned, saved back filthy and bone-cracking jobs.

Amazed Dane. Stupefied Dane. Electric over ignorance. Crude even among sailors, and like all sailors—as with other cynical forms of life—possessed of rough compassion.

"If you ever, ever, ever, ever, ever, ever a-bloody-gin step inside a line I will have your rotting guts for neckties ....," for, if Brace *did* step between line and rail, the sea would do the tearing.

Perturbed Dane. Red-faced. Melancholy—for at the end of three weeks it became clear that this young one was aboard to stay. If he was sometimes surly, he was also quiet and hard-working. The crew began to trust his beginner's job. The crew's acceptance meant that the old man would keep Brace. Captain Levere, mustang, kept his men. Since it was foolish to expect sense from the District, the crew assumed that to the south in the bustling offices which represented official mercy at sea, Levere commanded respect.

Seaman Glass took apprentice seaman Brace ashore and got him drunk on dime glasses of beer. It was a great success, and the next day Dane lovingly put Brace and his throbbing head to chipping paint on the bow; blazing sun heating the steel deck like a blowtorch.

"He don't respond to girls," Glass worried.

"... your kind of girls." Because of his tour of duty in the Far East, Lamp lived easily beside the oriental convictions of his steward, Amon; assuming that Amon had convictions, but Lamp worried over Jewishness and circumcision. Lamp cruelly rejected Glass's concern and supposed privately to yeoman Howard that Glass's pursuit of Portland bar girls had overtones of the occult, of dark deeds.

Yeoman Howard, dark, glandular and slim, who pursued constantly and with average success, once more mentioned to Lamp that he, Howard, already had a mother. Lamp clucked and fussed and mentioned to yeoman Howard that there would be a day of reckoning.

But then, Lamp clucked over all of them, those hard-ridden men who blinked in the summer sun and gradually returned to life and vigor. Except for Jensen who of course remained dead.

III

〰〰〰〰〰〰〰〰〰〰〰〰〰〰〰〰〰〰〰〰〰〰〰〰〰〰〰〰〰〰〰

HE HAD not been a fool, this dead man who would shortly become the nemesis of Ernie Brace. Jensen was an idealist with occasional poor judgment, and now he was a drowned idealist. In that past winter of treacherous seas there were occasional days of alarming calm. Downeasters know such days, when the North Atlantic seems gathering its forces to crack holes in the planet.

"Crazy?" In later days at the Base it would always be a young voice asking that. Only the young needed to ask.

"No," Lamp would say, and always he was serious. "Jensen was motivated. Very much. Also religious and good." By the time Lamp would tell the tale in its hundredth version, the figure of Cecil Jensen acquired the stature of major saint on Lamp's calendar.

"Poor judgment?"

"He might have made it."

That was true. At the time no one doubted that he would

make it, and Jensen (who was not religious, but who may have been good) most likely died while losing a bet with himself.

A day of calm saw him under. Those calms are, in their way, as treacherous as ice on superstucture. In some men they bring out the underlying romance, for seaman cynics are secretly romantic; believing the tradition of "you have to go out, you don't have to come back" . . . and let us say—for a chance—that the tradition is not a myth, but true.

Let us suppose that the weight of belief makes that awful proposition real and—although it will not here be held—that when the earth was railed by horizon, and flat to seamen's perceptions, that their belief made it flat—but in matters of the abstract. Well, then; true, no doubt, and if old men still believe the proposition, perhaps that is only because it is easy to believe from the depths of a comfortable chair.

Still, in some minds there is a difference between life and property. Jensen carried a submersible pump aboard *Adrian*'s ancient acquaintance, the fishing vessel *Louise*, on the day it sprang the last of its legendary leaks.

Adrian received the distress call while homeward bound from Rockland during one of those weeks God makes for drownings. Souls of the coast would remember that week as the week of the *Redstart*.

It was a terrible storm. Fishermen, lighthouse tenders, seamen and fishermen's wives from Newfoundland to Boston hovered helpless and voiceless and tense, with radio transmitters idle in their hands, as a nearly laconic voice from *Redstart* gave its last loran readings and was cut off in midsentence. Somewhere a cartographer placed a small red x on a chart. Cutter *Abner* beat a hopeless box search, struggling to stay alive, scaling the waves like a small white toy indifferently tossed into a riptide. On the coast, nine more crosses were planted along the cliffs, bearing the world's most lonely legend.

The storm was abating as cutter *Adrian* cleared the Rockland jetty. Enough weather remained to supply a sleigh ride. Rockland fell below the horizon at noon on a day when the gray light was absorbed into the gray sea so that only white spume blown from the tops of waves suggested the seam between wind and water. The voice from *Redstart* still echoed in the ears of the bridge gang. The trawler *Mary Rose* was now safe in Rockland, but it was little comfort that one crew was drying its socks while another crew was under.

Adrian skidded before a quartering sea, the steep swells piling and breaking with a rush on the fantail. The superstructure began to ice. Stanchions bulged with rime like stubby posts, and chains stretched between them as thick as dismembered arms linked in futility against the sea. The covered winch swelled with ice, bulking in the stern like a great dog huddled against the wind. Cold smoked from the sea, as if the waves were dry ice. It circulated through the ship and stretched even through the grates of the fiddley and into the engine room. Portside hatches were lashed partly open so that ice would not immobilize them.

Lamp fretted, made coffee and hot sandwiches, muttered either prayers or spells. The crew cursed with fatigue . . . a comfortable cursing because they knew the ship and this was not desperate weather. On the bridge Levere stood like a slumped, hawk-faced monument. He stood watch on watch as his ship added weight. *Adrian* had no steam hoses, but it had fire axes and hammers. As the storm blew itself out, the crew hacked ice. Then the radio popped, crackled, and through the heavy static the heavier voice of terror from the *Louise*. *Adrian* put the helm to port and headed into the sea.

That *Louise* was an abomination. It was a crate, a bucket, a ragtag of rust and frayed cable and wine dregs in the hold that could pickle an ocean or a wilderness or a nation of cod. From Gloucester to Portland it was scorned, sneered at, called the "Stinky Louise." *Adrian* had towed it three times in eighteen months. The thick-liquored voice of terror on the radio belonged to its Portuguese skipper who should have been in prison—and would have been had he not fled New Bedford. What crimes he committed ashore were not a seagoing concern. His crime against the *Louise* was astounding, for in three years he had taken a competent trawler and turned it into a rusting arcade of junk.

Louise's worn pumps were beginning to lose suction, the myriad leaks beginning to take on the authority of a policeman-executioner, and the liquored Portuguese and his liquored crew were imprisoned on the face of the sea.

Adrian's fourteen knots of flank speed were respectable in those waters. As the storm blew out and the speed rose, so did the anguished howling from the radio. The man was in a continuing seizure of fear, although if he had to take to his boats he was not in much trouble. The wind died, the swells began to knock down, and at worst he looked forward to an ugly night.

Of course, if his boats leaked worse than his trawler, the lot of them were dead. *Adrian*'s task was to make knots. The Portuguese's task was to pump and pray. It seemed a shame if he died, since he was going about the matter so badly.

They were a crew of sober men in the morning light. The sea was flat like a lake, and winter sun oiled its surface with a thin, red glow. The trim trawler silhouette changed from a high-riding, high-bowed sea boat before the morning sun. It looked like a pile of clutter on the horizon, like a barge on which spare parts of trawlers were randomly stacked. The bow was down, the stern riding low but enough exposed to make the wretched old crate look like a cigar butt wallowing in a gutter. *Louise*'s boats were tied alongside, and, as *Adrian* closed, the Portuguese and his crew took to them. They waved and hollered and wept. They shrieked until *Adrian* was within a hundred yards, coasting off the way, reversing screws so easily that not enough turbulence entered the calm water to as much as rock the boats.

The deck gang hauled them aboard. They came like rats, but without the sleekness of rats. A thin, urchin-like Spaniard babbled his mother's name and wept. An Italian, teeth chattering with cold, was pulled aboard and collapsed, uttering small puffs of shrieks. A beer tub of a German, leather-jacketed and swarthy, blubbered between thick lips. They smelled raw with booze, musty from sleeping for a week in their clothes. They stank like trash fish which someone had forgotten to throw to the gulls. They hugged icy stanchions, bundled onto the mess-deck to warm hands on coffee mugs and burn gullets with heavy slurping. Lamp tsked, served out food, crooned sympathy, and was obviously and thoroughly disgusted.

The abominable Portuguese would see the captain. Property was at stake. He climbed the ladder to the bridge, in a nervous state because he could not carry his coffee mug and still wring his hands. The Portuguese was thick, medium colored and of medium height. His entire sea ability was in the cut of his whiskers, which were as well greased as his pumps were not. Levere dismissed him to the main deck. The Portuguese rolled his eyes, gasped, incoherently babbled about seagoing codes. He stamped his feet like a child. He whined like a dog. He prayed to the Virgin and the devil.

Louise stood on the thin red water with gunnels still a foot above the surface. No decision was correct. *Adrian's* flotation would not support the trawler. If Levere came alongside and tied on, and if *Louise* slid, *Adrian* would be dragged over. Either that, or breaking lines might kill a man.

Yet, legally, Levere could not just allow the thing to die. It hovered on the sea, bowed like a tired workman, old and disgraced and unworthy. It had once been a strong, downeast work boat before the coming of the Portuguese. Now, in that romance of the seaman, it seemed that *Louise* wanted to die. The rusting winch and rusting cable lay in a last small chaos of despair. The rails were pocked deep, bleeding rust, and the thin pipe of the stack was disfigured where rust had flaked away and eaten out the top. Oil surrounded the gunnels to make the trawler a small blot on the rust-colored sea.

There was a hurried conference on the bridge, men muttering in the red dawn, casting pale shadows. Dane, Levere, Jensen. Howard jogged the dead helm and watched the drift. A quartermaster stood ready by the engine room telegraph and watched *Louise*.

"Not enough freeboard—submersible is ready—yes, well, but we must—of course—," they murmured, unsecretly hoping that *Louise* would take the decision from them. "A snipe—no, I'll go myself—life jacket—sure, sure, yes chum—back down after you're aboard, 'twill give you room—take a line— 'twould foul surely—I mean *carry* the thing, don't tie on—"

The crew silently stood at the rail, and silently aided Jensen. The Portuguese swore blessings, cried in the name of the pope. *Louise* shuddered but rode no lower.

That Jensen loved not life but living. In later days Lamp would say that he was spiritual, but spiritlike is how he looked. He made two trips, moved quickly, lithe in the bulky life vest, walking soft across *Louise*'s tumbled deck like a man treading on sharp pebbles. The submersible pump and the portable engine were heavy. He swung sideways. He was like a dancer portraying a crippled dream. His shadow was a wisp, faded and thin in the red light.

He approached the ladder that led below, looked about him, suspicious. *Adrian* was backing dead slow, the screw barely turning. Jensen shoved the submersible into the hatch, sat back on his heels, began to rig.

Dane descended from the bridge, tapped two seamen, and the three climbed into one of *Louise*'s boats. They shoved off and hovered between the two vessels. *Adrian*'s crew stood like a silent crowd along the rail. The Portuguese moaned.

Jensen rocked forward in his crouch, cursed, and with one smooth movement disappeared down the ladder. Dane's yell was blanked out by *Adrian*'s whistle. Levere's voice followed, stern, sad and urgent. The sounds were like sparks over the eternal hush of the sea.

Jensen was what? A fool? No one knew what Jensen saw,

what problem he faced that allowed him to make that decision. A discharge line snagged below *Louise*'s tumbled deck? In that dark space his voice echoed as he cursed the pump. Thumps, movement and his distant voice swearing . . . and then a shiver through the old trawler and it shifted deeper, hesitated, and then it was gulped.

It made a rapid hole in the sea as it slid. The rusted stack tipped slightly aft. There was a motion, a last movement; an attempt to retrieve life at the hatch . . . like the fluttering of a Mother Carey's chicken. The sea closed over the hole and the small boat carrying Dane and the seamen jumped and bucked. *Adrian* heeled. Waves splashed white, turned to ripples, fell back to red; and Dane—stony-eyed and unbelieving—returned to the ship and began systematically to kill the Portuguese. Levere and the deck gang pulled him off and locked the man in the safety of the lazarette. The Portuguese lived to make wine-soaked threats in the bars of Gloucester.

IV

〰〰〰〰〰〰〰〰〰〰〰〰〰〰〰〰〰〰〰〰〰〰〰〰〰〰〰〰〰〰〰

FLASHING NEON. Tailor-made blues. Dragons stitched in Chinese silk. Men and women laughing. Old faces. Young faces. Liberty.

"I want a transfer."

"You want another beer."

"Me, too," said Glass. "I want a transfer. To that *Andy* cutter down in Florida. I'm her next captain."

"A zoo. An absolute zoo." Brace's unremarkable features were pale. He seemed alarmed at the thought of another beer.

"Make bags of money being captain," Glass said. "Rake off the duty-free stores. Smuggle them to Cuba."

"You want to grow up," Howard told Brace kindly. "You want some sea time. Plus you want another beer."

"You got it made," Glass explained to Brace. "Me, I don't got it made. Not 'til I get next to those rich Cubans."

Red neon. Blue neon. Green neon. Tattoo neon. Light pulsing on the wan faces of bar girls with names that were fabulous: Jungle Judy, Radar the Snipe, Feelie.

"I never did anything to make Dane hate me."

"You never did nothing to make him love you."

"And there's rich Cuban ladies." Glass traced bountiful lines in the air with his hands. "We shouldn't never forget the ladies."

"Those ladies all smoke cigars," Howard told him.

The bars of Portland and the crusty waterfront, etched stark by sunshine where weathered gray boards of buildings stand like tall slats against the northeast wind; the bars which ruin "livers and lights" are places where crews unhunch from frustration, and drink against the illusion that fear is swept away.

Glass pointed out that if there were no bars there could be no waterfront missions. Unsaved souls would have to wander through mists more terrible than any imagined by the spiritualist Lamp.

Howard agreed. Howard said that bartenders were seminarians.

The crew went ashore and gradually got straight. Cutter *Adrian* slumbered on repair status. Cutters in Portsmouth, Boston and New Bedford took the duty. *Adrian* would cross courses with all of them during any year, small ships appearing ghostly from fog or mist, ships seen laboring in gale, and ice-covered from piling seas or from the black and howling mouth of storm; the new and competent 83 boats, the harbor and ocean-going tugs with towing screws to envy.

When the luck was thin, like ice in the knitted wool of a watch cap, the lousy cutter *Able*, of New Bedford, might be working alongside. *Able* was the broken strand in the hawser, the frail anchor line in the web of competence reaching from Argentia to Block Island. It was the ship that could not do, would not do, and which no one trusted. *Able* was sloppy and unhappy, perpetually changing officers and crew in a hopeless search for the combination that would make it a going concern.

In later years, forming one more grand theory of ships, Lamp would claim that when *Able*'s keel was laid the wives of seamen wept. "Boys, boys . . . I be double-dog-damn." According to Lamp, *Abner* was lucky, *Adrian* was well sinewed, and *Able* was jinxed.

"You got it made, chummy," Glass insisted. "You coulda been sent to *Able*. It's a sub."

"It's the navy has the submarines," Brace said wisely into his fourth fresh glass of beer.

"He means," said Howard, "that every time you see it you're surprised it's still afloat."

"I seen that thing in dry dock," Glass said. "It rusted the dry dock."

When you are young, experience seems to be a silk dragon or a cleverly stitched tiger on the sleeve of your tailormades. The ancient, ever-moving and murmuring sea pops small waves onto the beach through the summer calm. At Portland Head, the lighthouse is glazed cake-frosted white with sun, like a building from the Med plucked by Greek gods and transported.

Brace's instincts were sometimes good about the decks of a vessel on repair status, but they were lacking in other ways. He saw the sea and told Glass of a summer visit he had once made to Lake Michigan. Brace was not going to sea, and he was not going ashore with much success. The crew knew that repair status was more than luxury, it was luck. Brace was missing a bandstand opportunity.

The crew was woman-needful and brash. The men toured the bars, breathing the cool, stale beer smell of the bars that was as much their familiar as the sea. They engaged in territorial movement, like eager dogs wetting boundaries around hydrants. The crew was wary of foreign ships, of fancy and gorgeous uniforms that captured the entranced attention of the only women they knew.

"I hear your queen's got bow legs."

"Mate, you can't say that about our queen."

"There's this about your queen . . . ."

The fight, often joyous, with split lips and broken teeth.

"Honest, judge . . . "

"It was double jeopardy," Glass said. "I studied this."

"You missed one holy-roller of a fight," Howard told Brace.

"You miss just about everything, kid."

Each night Dane sat in a booth in the aft end of the bar, cool in khaki among the white uniforms or optional blue uniforms of his deck gang. Dane with his shack job, Florence, or "Flossy," drinking beer after beer as he spoke easily and with humor to the not unattractive, spoiled woman who drove expensive automobiles and enjoyed slumming. Outdrinking his deck gang, Dane seemed to be saying, was just one more boring part of his job.

"He won't leave us alone," Brace said. "Even ashore."

"He leaves me alone."

"You can always go to another bar."

"I got drunk once, really drunk," Brace said with deep and awful meaning. "If he keeps it up, I'm going to do it again."

Seaman Glass, recognizing a statement of experience that yeoman Howard at first missed, pursued the matter during the shore-going, and hot, and too short summer.

"He's deep," Glass told Lamp.

Lamp tsked to Amon. Amon's flat, Hawaiian face, which was principally Japanese, became studious in that way that happened when Lamp talked of mysteries. Amon may have thought Lamp in touch with old gods, or with living dragons wise with centuries; or, lighted by his name, thought him the one glow of sanity in Amon's otherwise closeted and lonely life. Amon, with an unease not otherwise known in New England, refused to wrestle with the source of revelation. He went to Howard instead.

"Brace is deep," Amon told Howard.

Brace was deep. Jensen was dead. Jensen's story, it was believed, was told. Brace's tale was only beginning, and Glass,

37

responding to the unlined forehead and occasional petulance of Brace, was shocked and morally twinged to learn that Brace had even a meager kind of history.

Lamp, in contrast, clucked to the crew over Brace's virtue. He hinted boldly to Dane that Brace would make a fine apprentice cook.

The crew eased mentally sideways, commented, judged and forgot. Brace's life story was not a sea story, but a small tale of the messdeck where Joyce, Majors and Conally sat to starboard, hunched and chomping, left thumbs—through habit—anchoring trays to table, forks stabbing from right hands with the delicate precision of men accustomed to eating rapidly below wildly skidding decks. The black gang—McClean, Masters, Wysczknowski, Racca and Fallon—chomped to port. At a small table near the ship's office the bridge gang of Rodgers, Chappel, James and Howard were a coffee-muzzling crew. The seamen, firemen, and *Adrian's* young pigeon, Brace, sat midships. Lamp stood like a wide-butted archangel wielding the hot sword of his galley fires. Amon was a constantly running thread tying all to the wardroom where Levere and Dane sat solitary.

The tale, transcribed from the beer-drinking confidences of Brace, through the twinge of Glass, and arranged into a morality play by Lamp, was not human drama until after a great deal of thought.

Brace had an older cousin—Jim or John, it makes no matter—and perhaps his last name was Smith; but as surely as old ships are reengined between wars, young men must have heroes.

"A jerk," Glass confided to Lamp. "He'd last five minutes in Boston."

This Jim or John was a midwestern miracle of a type so common in those parts that the miraculous is the standard of Rotarians. He raised 4-H cattle that won prizes, played basketball for a state university, and was healthy and blond and tanned and modest. He was, in sum, decent; a moral and right-thinking body, who, in the distance of time and miles translated through Brace's memory, was the ideal creature of conduct that Lamp applauded. On the surface, Brace's hero was sinless and guileless, and, if presented with his actual shape, Lamp would not have known what to do with him.

Brace was not a minister's son, except as all sons of southern Illinois in those days were spiritually sired by ministers. Brace was a son of dusty town squares, gravel roads, fields of corn and pumpkins, soybeans, tomatoes, sugar cane, hay, oats, rye, wheat, and the thin gleaning of daft certainty held by men who own clean barns, bulging red silos, sleek herds, chores, and pitchfork morality. Practically, Brace was the son of the high school bandmaster, a man who breathed the better quality of air, and who produced music that was mechanically sound. The father had a voice like the horns of Joshua. After a night in the bars, Brace claimed that if his old man had not done so much yelling it would have been easier to handle the big, fat, loud mouth of Dane.

"My pop wanted to be a doctor," Glass said, "but he's a yid. Works in a drugstore. Make a lot of money with a drugstore."

"At least he don't yell. Right?"

"He hates drugstores."

"Mine's a lawyer," a seaman said.

"A crook. I like you better, now," Glass told him.

"If you chase enough ambulances, you'll catch a few."

"Mine's a taxi-driving pimp."

"Mine's a dope."

"We didn't have one in our family," Howard admitted. "We were too poor."

"They're all crooks," Brace said knowledgeably into his beer. "I used to didn't know that."

Your seaman cynic, carrying in his heart that awful tradition that is not a myth, but true, is born of offenses rendered in the invisible world. One must go out, but the tradition does not require you to haul spurious cargo. The tradition is a jealous god. Your seaman cynic, that voluntary Jonah, may be forever offended by all other things, and that suits the tradition, just fine.

Brace's hero was three years his senior, experienced (as was Brace) at trumpeting in the band. Brace's hero did other and greater things: firing plinking rifles, grappling with dates, breeding cattle, driving at high speeds and shooting basketballs. He was blond and beautiful and, when Brace was not overcome with awe of his hero, Brace loved him. Brace, a son of copper-throated music and copper-fitted morals, looked up to a creature who lived comfortably with copper while having a wonderful time. Following the local ethic of seeking a profitable education, Brace arrived at the cow college where his hero was a star basketball player engaged in shaving points.

"A gorgeous con," Glass told Lamp. "Nobody got hurt. The team won and the gamblers won. You got to admire the set."

"Is that what they teach you in those fancy synagogues?"

"They teach delicatessen management," Glass said thoughtfully. "It just occurs, cook . . . this ship ain't kosher."

Texture fooled Brace. After years of being quietly followed as a hero, the man finally took an interest in Brace. There were motives, of course, but Brace did not even dream of such things. It seemed to him that he was magically launched into the deep meaning and pleasures of adulthood. Lovely young women talked to him. Young men, sensing him an important satellite to the charging and dribbling star, wished to be his friend. Without understanding the seediness of the situation, and without knowing how or why, Brace found himself in the role of an intermediary. Men visited his room and said they were alumni. The men left envelopes for the basketball player. Brace, stricken with uncritical worship, did not at first even try to understand.

"It's the drop man gets the trouble," Glass confided to Lamp. "Don't never get conned into taking the drop."

Lamp groaned and prophesied.

40

Understanding came slow. Through most of the season Brace cooperated, while running his small but increasing fund of knowledge through his conscience. He balked at the harm his mind was trying to discover; for heroes, after all, are not easy to come by, and young love suffers not from its lack of truth but from its lack of discrimination. He walked nighttime streets, stood in shadows before his hero's fraternity house, and, it may be, wept. When he finally understood the message of his conscience, he took that message back to the wise, older men who had given the conscience to him in the first place.

Brace talked to his father. His father spoke in broad and certain tones like the voice of a trombone. His father said that Brace was doing the right thing. His father said that Brace made him proud. His father told Brace to take his information to the minister.

The minister blinked with emotion, as if struck in a mortal place by a beatitude. He shot his cuffs, adjusted his tie, fondled a hymn book, gave a brief prayer of thanks. The minister said that Brace was doing the right thing. God was glad. The minister said he would speak to the basketball coach.

The basketball coach towered above Brace. He laid manly hands the size of hoops on Brace's shoulders. The coach thanked Brace for doing the right thing in the name of clean sportsmanship.

Brace's hero disdained him. When Brace phoned the lovely young women, with the lovely, tight-fitting angora sweaters, their roommates said that they were not in. His new men friends greeted him coldly, or not at all. Alumni stopped visiting. Through the rest of the season Brace attended the games, watched wins by narrow margins flash triumphantly on the glowing scoreboard. In the spring, his hero graduated and was hired at a high salary by a professional team.

Brace's father, this time in a voice like a tuba, decided that in the following year Brace would attend a smaller college nearer to his home.

It would take nearly another year, a year of loneliness that accumulated through silences and avoidance and summary conversations, before Brace understood that every man he knew detested him. His womenfolk could not help. They knew nothing of the affair. Brace's instincts told him that it was best left that way.

He felt that the world had stumbled. Even the fields, the cropland, the certainty of green and growing things seemed frail and dying. The fields looked like gigantic boxes or crates, heavy with vegetables that were already packed and were for sale.

It is "as rough as a cob" to admit that you no longer have a home. Regret combines with fear when you know you must leave. With some men there is only one way to get the job done. Brace got drunk, truly drunk, really drunk. He puked, passed out, slept, woke, showered, drank coffee and enlisted.

V

A SET of dungarees ask a good number of washings to make them comfortable. Splotches of red lead, paint, tar, bloodstains from cracked knuckles, frays, patched tears from mistakes with tools, scuffs from loading stores, oil spots on bell bottoms, and a seat worn smooth while the man is pulling an oar in the small boat—introduce a set of dungarees to these influences, add rust that works into the weave to grate and loosen cotton fibers, and the most ironclad outfit works into a liveable, seagoing rig.

By August Brace's dungarees were beginning to fade while *Adrian* became brighter. Coiled heaving lines dangled monkey fists from straightened and painted rails. The davits stood like large, inverted hooks with a new small boat, lapstraked and white, snagged between them as rigidly fixed as the sacred cod. Hot updrafts blasted through the fiddley grates as the engines went on the line, rumbling, rough, then smoothing from their godlike belches into a civilized mutter of controlled power, as the engineman, and electrician Wysczknowski, adjusted and puttered and persuaded in low tones. The regulated flow of fuel and lube oil and cooling water spoke in the gush of the overboard discharge, and the black gang appeared abovedecks in the shocking sunlight like old monks from cells after prayer and fasting.

" . . . . B–race . . . . "

"Get crackin', get crackin'."

Brass ports gleamed and glowed and smouldered like fixed halos, showing here and there a white streak of unwiped polish. Bronze nozzles, straight-stream and fog, were shadowed in the sun between the bleached white layers of new firehose packed above smooth, gray-painted decks where blisters and bubbles of rust, scraped away, would not bleed hints of mortality until December. The rust lay waiting in its coffers, as imminent as ice, immoral as a government.

"Follow through. Follow through. Follow through, you—cow milker."

On the pier Brace heaved the line, the arc high and slanting at upright orange life-ring targets staggered to a distance of a hundred feet. The targets were like small, round mouths of scorn. Brace heaved the line for a full working day.

"I got no wrists left."

"Nor ever will," Glass told him, "as long as you keep turnin' 'em."

While Howard watched, Dane nagged and chafed and sent the wrestler-shaped, Indian-blooded third class bosun Conally to stand behind Brace like a vulture.

"Like boxing," Conally told Brace. "Start from your toes, not your knees." Conally heaved a line into the mouth of the far target. "Lay your coil smooth—smooth." He turned his back to the targets and flipped the line over his shoulder to strike the center of the nearest one.

"It's a circus act," Brace said.

"He stinks," Conally told Dane.

"Clean him up."

"No liberty," Conally told Brace. "Until you can heave the line."

"That's restriction. You got no authority to do that."

"See our man on the bridge. See Levere. Take your lawyer with you."

Brace heaved the line. In a week the arc flattened and the monkey fist was hitting the sides of the rings. Half the throws were getting through.

"Another week," Conally told Dane.

"Is he tryin'?"

"He's tryin'."

"Give him a little run ashore."

"Go do whatever you do," Conally told Brace. "Don't bump your arm."

Brace went ashore, returned sober, to heave the line.

"I ain't the only guy on this deck gang," Brace complained to Howard.

Howard laid a coil and snaked the line toward the far target. The monkey fist hit two feet short and bounced against the target base. Howard laid a second coil and snaked the line through the target.

"It don't pay to forget."

"You hit it the second time," Brace said.

"From solid decks. This pier's not moving." Howard laid another coil and began to practice. Radioman James, looking meager and remote and pale, with nearly whitened hair and washed gray eyes, was passing from the Base back to the ship. He stopped, watched, silently picked up a line. He made a throw, bounced the line from the edge of a target, turned to Brace. "Your coil's got no spring. Lay it like this . . . "

"Don't teach him nothing fancy," Howard said. "Let him learn the plain way first."

If, from New Bedford, the lousy cutter *Able* could not tow the plug from a bathtub, that was all the more reason why deck seamen aboard *Adrian* and *Abner* learned to stand backup to a fireman's steaming watch. Firemen learned the helm, and how to make ready the decks to get underway. Yeoman Howard was third quartermaster, while senior quartermaster Chappel could type. Gunner's mate Majors, less than blessed to belong to a crew that could not, with the three-inch-fifty gun, hit the broad side of a continent at five hundred yards, acted as third bosun to Dane and Conally. Equipment was hard to come by. A less awful tradition said, "Patch it up and make it do," but even a frugal Treasury Department was generous in the matter of towline.

It came aboard in the first week of August. A new, enormous coil, spiky with small fibers poking through the lay like the remaining bristles on a balding brush. The line was stiff, hard, dry, waxy, unsalted, unbleached, unstained with rust, unmarked by chafing gear, and perhaps, even to Brace, it was beautiful.

Lamp appeared on the fantail like a priest investing a new house or enterprise. He tsked and worried, sat in the sun like a great, sweating slab of ham. The huge bundle was broken and the line laid the length of the port main deck, around the house, down the starboard side, and back up to port. Seamen walked the line, hand-rolling away fistlike loops, sweating and grunting, backs strained against the weight.

"The luck is turnin', boys."

"Which-a-way, cook, which-a-way?"

"Don't scorn luck, boys."

"Which way, cook?" Levere, hawk-faced, French-faced, and taciturn as a Scot, appeared on the boat deck to watch the investiture.

"How easy it works," Lamp exclaimed. "It's stiff but willin', cap."

"It's just well packed."

"Don't scorn luck, cap."

"Nobody does," Levere told him. "You ought to give a good deal of thought to that, cook."

Howard, watching from the pier, his badge of office the immaculate white hat rolled and bleached over dark, brief waves of hair, stood beside the short, bear-shaped second engineman, Fallon, who had a reputation for smart hands; an instinct for machinery that Lamp could somehow explain by talking of Peter the Great. Fallon conversed with pumps, complained to sweat joints, held arterial arguments with webs of piping. He stood like a keg, parting the light breeze that blew down the pier between *Adrian* and *Abner*—heavy-browed, round-faced, and with grease-stained hands—perturbed to hear the unnatural squawk of gulls and the alien-whispering wind.

"We got orders for Jensen's replacement," Howard told him. "From cutter *Aaron*. A chief engineman name of Snow."

"He won't beat Jensen, chum. What kinda foolish name is Snow?"

"An easy-to-spell name," Howard told him. "You on top of it down there?"

"We just waitin' to get reported on the line."

"Snow shows up next week."

"We'll wait," Fallon said. "Belowdecks is clean. Be a shame to mess it up by usin' it." He sniffed suspiciously at the breeze, like a man divining for oil while suspecting he will strike water.

"If we got a week, let's spend it. I want that new kid broken in."

"I'll mention it to Dane."

"Snow? What's his first name?"

"Edward."

"A Limey. We went for years without a chief in that engine room—an' without a Limey, neither."

"He'll spend his time in the wardroom."

"Not a chance," Fallon said morosely. "We waited this long. You can just bet your uppers that Levere has found hisself a hotrock."

Across the pier, the crew of *Abner* did its devotions before a new bundle of line. Seamen walked loops, snipes came blinking from below, or from the messdeck. Some of the men carried coffee mugs. They gabbled, slurped, chewed on sandwiches. The bridge gang clustered on the boat deck like a makeshift choir at a Sunday school picnic, a choir ambiguous in the face of hot dogs, pie, and amazing grace.

"It starts again," said Fallon.

"*Abner* takes the duty Monday," Howard told him. "Us, we still got a little over a week."

Howard spoke to Dane, who spoke to Fallon, who passed the word to Brace. When Brace understood that he was ordered to stand cold-iron watch and take instruction on steaming, he went to Dane, complaining bitterly, his mouth running hot with adolescent vigor. He was shocked to find his words probing beneath Dane's professional cussedness, to enter the true cussedness of a land where no grown man would ever want to visit.

Dane, squat, froglike, less gracious than a crocodile, his thin lips as tight with anger as his shape was tight with rheumatism, shoved Brace into the ship's office.

"I don't want to see this punk for a week," Dane told Howard. "Full duty below. Watchstanding and bilges. Lots of bilges."

Brace stood, like a man immersed in memory. He murmured. "*What?*"

"I got rights."

"You got hoof-and-mouth disease," Howard told him kindly. "Your big hoof in your fat mouth. I keep telling you."

"Restriction," Dane said. "If I catch him ashore, I'll gut him."

"You've been having a wonderful summer aboard," Howard said when Dane was gone. "You're going to love the bilges."

Brace stood protesting that a seaman was not a fireman, that black was not white, and that people couldn't just go *changing* things. Howard said that this was not Illinois; Brace said, what did that mean; and Howard understanding on some inarticulate level that the youthful Brace was perfervidly asking for order in both the visible and invisible universes, said that as soon as

Brace learned that he was a crew member of *Adrian*, and not just a prima donna ex–cow milker striking for seaman, then the happier all of them would be.

Brace went to the engine room, to the sweet, slightly rotten and clammy odor of the bilges where red lead never completely dried, to the sure and perfectly cutting scent of ozone rising hot in the nose, to air layered with the thin and oily taste of diesel, and the smartly grabbing stench of wet valve packing. His thin nose wrinkled, but he discovered that belowdecks he was never bothered by Dane. Brace was loading a cargo of auxiliary information. The engine spaces were in good order. The enginemen could afford to go easy.

"I like it down there," Brace confided to the sweating and bustling Lamp. "They got a different attitude."

"Because of Jensen. He was good." In anticipation of *Adrian*'s return to duty, Lamp was heavy shouldered about the galley, mixing meringue, as though a special treat of lemon pie was a ritual end to summer.

"Snipes is always late getting the word," Glass said in passing.

"You are a bad man," Lamp groaned. "Bad."

"Jensen made a mistake," Howard said from his position by the coffee urn. "And Glass, you just now almost made one."

"Be careful with your mouth," Lamp said. "I feel it, boys. The luck is skiddy."

Things (as if they were endorsing Lamp's bleak guess) began to disappear. The key to an ammunition locker checked out missing, to be found two days later by gunner Majors in a pocket he had delved into a dozen times. Majors ran his inventory and it was intact. Amon, always precise, could not locate twenty pounds of coffee; to find it, after chattering bursts of frenzy, nestled for no scrutable reason in a locker in the wardroom. Howard searched desperately for a lost requisition which, the following week, appeared like a flick of sorcery between unused pages of the ship's log.

In later years while cooking at the Base, Lamp would vow

that nothing had been exactly unusual, nothing exactly wrong. There had been only the feeling that gravity had slipped and time was laughing. Events, normal enough when isolated, had piled up, jumbled and tumbled together, swept back and forth like a lost net washed onto a rocky, pooling beach.

As Lamp revealed that Pluto was conjuncting in some dismal way with Venus and the local newspaper spoke of sunspots—while reporting that the nation's president had lost another golf ball in a sand trap—Brace received a "Dear John" letter from a teenager named Mona. Glass gossiped to Howard that while on midwatch he saw Brace walk silently to the rail and drop a flat object which plunked into the dark water.

A piece of waste materialized in a rebuilt check valve. There was a revolution in Chile. Engineman-designate Racca, with luck as bad as his bad mouth, and ashore with a deep thirst, encountered a young person named Peak's Island Sally and a subsequent dose of penicillin, both for the very first time.

"Boys, boys. Boys, boys."

Chief engineman Edward Snow reported aboard a day early to the consternation of a black gang still smarting with a plugged valve; the same day that Brace left the engine room, and the day when the phone on-shore connection failed for two hours, only to be discovered when a messenger arrived from the Base with a testy TWX message from First District saying that Operations was trying to make a routine call to Levere.

"Skiddy, boys. I be double-dog-damn if it's good nor bad. Just backwards."

The ordinarily smart-moving Indian Conally sprained an ankle and hobbled in tape like a wounded racehorse. An admiring senator spoke of proud traditions and of cutting the service's budget. The commandant sent an all-units memorandum to express the hope that each man would do his best; and cutter *Abner*, showing its stern, steamed toward a mess that would soon work out to be one of the biggest flukes in the history of line-breaking.

VI

〰〰〰〰〰〰〰〰〰〰〰〰〰〰〰〰〰〰〰〰〰〰

CHIEF ENGINEMAN Edward Snow was small and quick, and only a little effeminate. He leered displeasure from a raised left eyebrow instead of hollering; and he took a tough and competent black gang and made it better.

"We'll not do it that way, lads."

Snow moved as accurately as a dipper gull, but he looked like a trim, khaki-colored towhee. By many pounds, and two or three inches, he was easily the shortest and lightest man aboard. Even the compact Amon seemed like a lumbering two-decker bus in comparison. Snow's feet never tapped with impatience, but he caused others' feet to tap as they pondered his administration. Fallon swore that Snow had typical brown English hair and was a socialist. When Howard pointed out that Fallon had never met a brown Englishman, socialist or not, Fallon muttered curses.

"He took down Jensen's watchstanding orders."

"The Ark of the Covenant," Glass said. "Yids understand these things."

"Don't make jokes."

Snow pulled piping and wiring diagrams from the files. In league with Fallon and electrician Wysczknowski, he traced the systems and altered the diagrams. Cutter *Adrian* had been replumbed and rewired so many times that the diagrams were a cat's-paw of revision. Quartermaster Chappel and yeoman Howard knew less about a drafting board than they knew about an abacus, but they began learning to draft. Revised schematics slowly began to stack up in the ship's office, and even more slowly to appear in freshly redrawn form. Chappel and Howard struggled and cursed. *Adrian*'s twin, cutter *Abner*, was at sea and equally struggling. Seaman apprentice Brace was tilted slaunchways from another encounter with Dane and—because of the lost Mona, or made lonely by the dying summer—was constructing a new hero.

"All hands belowdecks must memorize these diagrams," Snow told Howard. "Work with great care."

"It's the only way you can work, when you don't know what you're doing."

"You are receiving a large favor," Snow told him. "Few quill-drivers ever learn how to draft."

With *Adrian* on standby, the crew found itself testy after a summer of inaction. Men grumbled that since they could not go ashore it was foolish to hang against the pier. They muttered against the judgment of First District Operations as they followed the steadily increasing troubles of cutter *Abner*.

"Levere already asked," radioman James told an assembly on the messdeck. "Operations won't give us a proceed-and-assist." To Lamp he said, "I thought *Abner* was supposed to be lucky."

"The sea's not running hard, boys."

"That's blamed small luck."

"It's touchy, boys. It's touchy. Don't think bad thoughts."

Across the pier, and on the seaward side, where the familiar shape of *Abner* had seemed rooted during the summer, there now lay only the long perspective of distance.

The harbor still sparkled with sunlight, the inner islands were black, tree-covered and faraway humps, while clean-lined and freshly painted Norwegian freighters stood at the docks beside rusty Panamanian buckets, scarred coastal tankers, trim Britons, Canadians and a small white-and-green Irishman sparkling with pride and polish. Spectral French and Italian death ships mouldered against the docks like ghosts suffering extreme unction through the sacramental wine in their scuppers, rust in their bilges, and the oil that enclosed their hulls. Gray and white American tankers flew snapping corporation colors from their masts like small testimonials to efficiency; and, hanging like spiders in great clusters of drying nets, the ever present trawlers were aromatic with sweat and sun and fish as men forked the catch from the holds like farmers pitching hay—while, in the channel, yachts and lobster boats moved like a swirl of gnats above the face of a drowsing absolute.

Cutter *Abner*, en route to the grounds, laid line aboard the trawler *Ezekiel*, disabled with a cracked piston while inbound with a full catch packed beneath rapidly melting ice. Glass, standing bridge watch on the moored *Adrian*, was joined by Howard who was taking a break. Glass intermittently checked *Abner's* progress. He switched the radio to the working frequency of 2694.

"They'll save the load," Howard said, "if he don't break his seal too often staring down his hatch."

"We've raised to eight knots," said the static-crackling voice of *Abner's* captain. "How are you riding, cap?"

"Raise it more if you wa-nt-a." *Ezekiel's* radio was stronger than the rig on *Abner*. "This load ain't too thrifty."

"We'll stay with eight," *Abner* crackled.

"No sea to speak of," said Glass, "if they're shagging it that fast."

"They better shag it fast. They're sitting on a perfume factory."

It was then that Brace, passing a gallon of paint from the

53

main deck to a man on the boat deck, learned that you never lift an open can of paint by the bale.

Glass switched the set back to the faintly popping watch frequency. Through the open hatch, and distant, sounded the snap of the commission pennant, while from the buoy yard a crane groaned and whirred. An engine chugged and idled in the small boat basin. There was a thump, a small confusion of voices, a shout, and then whoops and hollers of laughter which gave way to a heavily trudging step along the main deck. Silence accompanied the walker, and then low laughter resumed as a thin, birdlike whistle of amazement seemed to nudge the heavy steps forward and up the ladder to the bridge.

Brace stepped through the hatch wearing a single wrinkle on his otherwise smooth forehead, and doused with green paint splashed in his hair, across one cheek, and saturating his shirt like a slick lustre of green blood. The paint ran the length of one leg and colored a shoe. Brace looked like a member of the walking wounded, but, though bowed, stood as unrepentant as a cannibal unfairly baptised by a zealot.

"I have," Brace said, "three years, seventeen days . . . . " He stooped forward like an old man to look at Glass's wristwatch, " . . . eleven hours and thirteen and a half minutes to pull in this fun house. I want a transfer to the engine room."

"That's the way all thirty-year men talk," Glass said. "Me, I ain't a thirty-year man. I'm putting in time 'til the Mafia calls."

"Stop dripping," Howard told Brace.

"Let him drip if he wants," Glass said. "How much worse off can he get?"

"A request mast," Brace said. "I want to change my rate to the engine room."

Howard stared at Brace and seemed to be giving the matter his deepest attention. "There shouldn't be any trouble in getting a mast," he said in tones that displayed great thoughtfulness. "I hear it climbing the ladder."

Dane's slow step was accompanied by puffs of deep breath

drawn against rheumatism, and they made mere doom seem like a cheap and silly thing. Dane appeared in the hatch that led to the wing and he squinted. His eyes widened and stared, froglike. His thin mouth was as tight and straight as any line on Howard's beginning diagrams. Dane blinked, made motion to move onto the bridge, stopped.

No one, in Howard's memory, had ever before seen Dane speechless. The radio crackled. The commission pennant popped. The indifferent idling of the engine in the small boat basin smoothed and rose with a controlled growl as the boat set off on harbor patrol.

"Illinois," Dane whispered hoarsely, "I wisht they sent the cow, instead." He stepped through the hatch and onto the bridge. At first he looked both awed and reverent. Then he eyed Brace in the way that a hungry man might view a pork chop, but when he spoke his voice was low and seemed nearly kind. "I don't want to know how you did it," he told Brace. "I don't want to know why you did it . . . " He slowly straightened like an inflatable raft filling and stretching toward shape. Howard and Glass watched, backed away, fascinated by the swelling chest beneath the khaki shirt as Dane gulped air to roar from full lungs and a fuller heart—

"But why in the name of God and the Holy Clap did you track it around!"

The radio crackled. The departing boat's engine was a rhythmic and diminished hum. In the buoy yard the crane snuffled and clanked. Brace opened his mouth to protest, looking like a man trying to spit out too much air as he faced a hurricane wind.

The radio popped, fizzled, settled to a hum as somewhere at sea a transmitter opened:

"Priority. Priority," said a nervous, frightened voice from *Abner.* "Nan-mike-fox from nan-mike-fox-two-one . . . priority, priority."

Howard stood stunned. Brace drooped. Howard looked at

Glass, at Dane, and saw their shocked and temporarily vacant faces.

"Calling Operations."

"That's their radioman, Diamond. I'd know that dago's voice anywhere. That's a tough dago."

"Stay on top of it," Dane told Glass. "I'll be back as soon as I get this kid to pasture." He looked at the radio, which, to all but Brace, suddenly seemed like a lethal gray box of fright. He looked once more at Brace, then at paint spills on the matting of the bridge, splashes on the wing, and pools between cleats on the ladder. Brace, his moment of defiance passed, stood miserable. He looked like a half-finished but brightly colored crayon drawing.

Glass pressed a buzzer, bent forward to a voice tube. "We need you on the bridge, cap."

Dane took a deep breath, sighed, nodded to Brace. "You don't clean yourself until after you clean the starboard side. If you get crackin', you'll finish sometime this week."

"A tough dago," Glass muttered. "He ain't scared of nothing."

"He's scared of something." Dane absentmindedly gave Brace a small shove, saw green paint on his fingers, wiped the paint on Brace's shirt. "Get movin'."

Some days later, with *Abner* once more hanging on the opposite side of the pier, Howard talked to his best friend, *Abner*'s yeoman Wilson. Wilson was a large man with an ordinarily chalky face, and his voice, ordinarily gruff, was still thin with a particular memory.

"The helm couldn't have been locked tighter if it was lashed," Wilson said. "He had this crazy quick-release gear that came down over the helm like a pair of hands. I never felt so spooky in my life."

If a dinosaur had appeared at prayer in Saint Peter's, it would have been only a little more remarkable than discovering a lobsterman underway seventy miles offshore and vaguely headed in the direction of Georges.

"It was wallowing along, making maybe one knot," said Wilson. "We'd been towing *Ezekiel* for an hour. The old man had just settled on the towing speed."

In the afternoon sun, but with rolling mist up to *Abner's* stern, the small lobsterman was like a remote, black and gray pinprick of solitude struggling toward the mist. Among those hermits who deal in lobster, those men who seek remoteness and silence as well as a catch, this lobsterman seemed hard-headedly intent on insisting that one could not have enough of a good thing. The boat rose and fell easily in a light swell. As cutter *Abner* approached, some quirk of monkish defiance seemed to turn the lobsterman across *Abner's* path. As the vessels closed, a collision course developed. *Abner* took off speed. The lobster boat moved as purposely across *Abner's* bow as might a small animal pursue its excursions across the face of a mountain and under a formation of clouds.

"No one aboard," Wilson said. "Our cap put over the small boat and our guys ran it down."

The lobsterman, locking his helm in the bleak waters that splashed against the dark islands that surrounded his trade, setting his speed like a hum to underline his solitude, had been pulling traps. The slowly moving boat closed on the marker buoy. The lobsterman plucked the line from the water and took a turn on a cleat. The low speed of the boat broke the trap loose from the bottom. The technique saved some hauling, and it was common practice; but this time the man missed the cleat, doubtless had a turn of line over his hand, and the trap dragged him overboard. The boat, still under way, left him struggling in icy water, in combat with his high boots; a struggle that was small in that wet vastness that closed, empty and complete, over the final solitude.

"We had such an eerie feeling," Wilson said, "but the worst of it came later."

News of "the worst of it" spread to *Adrian* like the chill of ice fog rolling toward and over an anchored vessel. News of "the worst of it" traveled to the Base, thence across the million-dollar bridge to the bars of Portland, along the piers and into the trawlers, the lobster boats, and, subsequently, south through the fishing fleet. It became a sea story. There was no conversation so light, so ridiculous or so gay that could not be stilled by mention of the lobster boat *Hester C.*

Lamp's leonine head was filled with auguries. He told stories of the Bermuda Triangle. He talked to the hobbling Indian Conally, asking after ancient spirit tales that might help him form a complete theory.

"Maybe some of the old people know," Conally said doggedly. "I never paid no attention to that stuff."

" 'Tis coming on to winter."

Dane, who had seen a thousand frightened seamen, was unimpressed. He blustered and threatened.

Howard reluctantly admitted that he felt the gray chill. Glass sarcasmed at himself for a sudden urge to speak Yiddish.

Brace, both then and earlier, was occupied with other matters, matters so personal and intense that no sea story could penetrate his unhappiness.

With stiff green hair and stiff dungarees, Brace cleaned paint for three days in the sun. At night he was allowed to remove his clothes and sleep in a paint-stained bunk. Dane was scrupulous. Not a fleck of paint escaped him. On a dozen occasions Brace swore that he was finished, and Dane found more paint —between the grill of the ladder, on the underside of a rail, spotted beneath the mats on the bridge, or tracked to other parts of the ship on the clothes or shoes of seamen. At the end of three days even Dane was content. Brace, unable to accomplish a personal cleanup, begged Amon for help, and Amon shaved Brace's head.

"There are such tales on the Grand Banks," chief engineman Snow mentioned with little interest to second engineman Fallon. "Come, lad, when we plot the bilge piping, the job is complete."

"The lobster boat was nearly out of fuel," *Abner's* yeoman

Wilson told Howard. "Been wallowing along for two or three days. His lobsters was dead but not stinkin'.'"

Abner had streamed grapples and gone through the necessary hours and motions of a hopeless box search. The ice in the trawler *Ezekiel's* hold was melting.

"We rigged a short tow aft of *Ezekiel*," Wilson told Howard. "Put a seaman aboard. All the kid had to do was lock down that helm and keep watch."

Abner, according to yeoman Wilson, settled into a straight double tow toward nightfall. A double tow was not common, but it was something *Abner* had done a dozen-twenty-times before. The deck force was short one watchstander because of the man on *Hester C*. Still, enginemen and firemen were running two on, four off. An eight- to ten-knot breeze rose. The tows rode well and *Abner* maintained speed.

"We were just changing watch for the mid," Wilson said. "That kid on the lobster boat got the engine started somehow. He dropped the tow and came kiting around *Ezekiel's* stern like he had a pocketful of pus. Ran the boat alongside, eyes bulging like a cod, and yelling that the boat was haunted. We lost an hour rerigging the tow."

"And that's when the *Clara* caught fire?"

"No," Wilson shook his head in wonderment. "The *Clara* didn't catch fire until they were relieving the four-to-eight. I was aboard that bumboat at the time.

"It was just nothing, at first," Wilson said after a moment spent thinking. "We rode for nearly an hour, me, and this seaman with his teeth chattering and pretending like he was brave. The dead lobsters were sloshing around in the well. We couldn't run the engine because of the low fuel. It was just real quiet, and the running lights were dirty and dim and things were all shadowy." Wilson looked at Howard, knowing that Howard had already heard the story, thinking, perhaps, that Howard would say that the story was only crazy.

"This hand came up over the transom," Wilson said. "It just

hung there for maybe thirty seconds, just pale and graspy, and then it slipped away. I ran aft and there wasn't nothing. No splash. That kid seaman started to cry. Ten minutes later the hand came back again. I ran forward and started leaning on the whistle to signal for a stop." Wilson looked ashamed, and then indignant. "We were only trying to help," he said. "Trying to get the boat back in so at least his old lady could sell it. That guy was dead. He didn't have any right to do that. He didn't have any right at all."

VII

‿‿‿‿‿‿‿‿‿‿‿‿‿‿‿‿‿‿‿‿‿‿‿‿‿‿‿‿‿‿‿‿‿‿‿

AT EACH nightfall the gray chill seemed to move like the whisking touch of a spirit hand across *Adrian.* As standing lights flared against the slowly encroaching dusk that layered with the cold and colder-growing diminishment of a waning summer, men chatted beside the galley, or walked the decks, or laundered, played cards, laughed and told stories. Commercial radios on the messdeck and in the crew's compartment were turned higher. The compartments were filled with the voices of young women, touted as "hot chicks" by a local disc jockey who praised songs of love and its unavoidable sadness. The gray chill, experienced at outwaiting eons of illusions, dwelt like an ice-covered boulder planted at the foot of the gangway.

At 2200 hours, dead center in the eight-to-twelve watch, the stories faltered, the flaring and somehow suddenly beautiful incandescent lights went out, and the red nightlights were switched on. They signaled the approach of grayness. Watchstanders on the bridge and in the engine room turned the incandescent lights up in those spaces, rolled pencils across the faces of log sheets, listened suspiciously to normal sounds; but through the rest of the ship the red lights threw pale shadows that grew increasingly grotesque.

"Nobody's talking," Mother Lamp confided seriously to Howard. "It's like the boys are pretending t'isn't there."

"Maybe it's behind your shoulder, cook."

"You've got a smart mouth," Lamp said, "but you're not smart about this. This has the same feel of something that happened once in Hong Kong."

"There aren't enough Chinese in Hong Kong to match the number of times I've heard about Hong Kong."

"You haven't heard this." Lamp seemed attentive to an inner voice, a communication rising from some heretofore great void, the cold of which only he had suspected. He shook his red-blond-haired head, looked at Howard like a mother doing her best to dote on an idiot child. Then his face changed. He was nearly timid, certainly sad. "I know you don't like me much. It's okay. Nobody hired you to."

"I just give you a hard time, cook." Howard was caught with the unease of a man who has stumped his toe on a fact. "Sometimes you make too much of things."

"Sometimes I do," Lamp said. "So do you."

"We all do," Howard said magnanimously.

"No, we don't. Lots don't. But you do, and I do."

"What happened in Hong Kong?"

"You're right," Lamp said. "I'm making too much of a thing." He refused to tell the story. The refusal, with even less precedent than men walking on unfrozen water, pressed Howard into silence.

The week seemed saturated with gray chill and green paint. Cutter *Abner* sent no messages about the haunt. That was left to the fate-stricken skipper of *Ezekiel* who was sitting above a load of fish packed in rapidly decaying ice. The skipper talked to fishermen friends on the radio as he watched *Abner*'s stern disappear at flank speed to assist the burning *Clara.* "Won't even do for fertilize'," *Ezekiel's* skipper said. "Going to try to hang on, chum, but I make it that we'll have to pitch the whole catch overboard. We got this jinx boat swingin' alongside." Long before *Abner*, trailing its string of refugees, made the Portland Lightship, the nub of the story and its amplifications had entered the bars.

"They were heads-up and lucky," *Abner's* yeoman Wilson told Howard. "The fire in the *Clara* started in wiring in the engine spaces. They got it out, but they had structural damage aft."

"It caused some heat aboard our ship," Howard told him. "The new kid got a burn."

Brace, wearing the aroma of turpentine, and with stiff green hair, came off the four-to-eight and went to the messdeck to eat before making his renewed attack on spilled paint. In the wardroom which lay forward of the messdeck on the starboard side, with the ship's office sitting between, Levere, Dane and Snow discussed timber for emergency shoring. Dane sat toad-silent, listening, respectful of Snow. To the surprise and provisional despair of some, Dane seemed to like Snow completely. Lamp bustled about the galley to port where he made watchstander chow for Brace and engineman striker McClean. Amon peeled spuds and kept an attentive ear cocked toward the wardroom. Brace arrived with a ladder-thumping stomp, intended, no doubt, to announce that—green paint or not—he remained his own man. He drew coffee, sat in his customary place, and slurped in a seamanlike manner; stolid, nearly, as if the presence of a wrinkle on his forehead gave him the responsibility for new reserve. His hands trembled only slightly.

"The problem ain't technically storage," said Dane. "But where can we store it so we can get at it fast?"

"Not below, of course," said Snow. "To be rapidly available it must be abovedeck."

"Got to keep the working decks clear."

"Paint it against rot," Levere said. "Cut it to fit as a false deck for the flying bridge. Secure it with light cable and quick-release gear."

"That'll work. Now, how do we get hold of it?"

"There is salvageable scrap stacked behind the Base," said Snow.

From the galley came the distant voice of Lamp asking watchstander Brace if there were later news on *Clara*.

Brace's voice, filled with hatred of paint, with frustration of green hair and stiff clothes, with anguish over the unfair death of dreams, and certainly with the violence that attends confusion, answered in a voice of low and malicious satisfaction.

"That's one we won't have to haul. That one isn't going to cause anybody much more trouble."

In the wardroom there was momentary silence.

"Excuse me, Captain. Chief." Snow picked up his coffee mug, stepped through the office and onto the messdeck, a man walking casually on an errand only a little less innocuous than the Creation. Like an inquiring, small brown towhee, he stopped before Brace and peered. Then, with distaste for either the man or the job, he backhanded Brace across the mouth. The blow seemed casual, light, and yet Brace's head was thrust as sharply as if he had been hit by a hatch cover. Brace recovered, started to rise, sat back down and looked upward at Snow through shock, as if questioning Snow's fortitude and his own.

"A man had to do that for me once, lad. I think to pass on the favor."

Brace sat dumb. Snow absentmindedly walked to the coffee urn, refilled his mug, and stepped back into the wardroom. Engineman striker McClean, normally quiet to the point of near idiocy, his long mulatto head and his jug ears as incongruous in society as his narrow fingers and thin wrists were around machinery, understood. "You've never seen a fire at sea," he told Brace.

"Please excuse it, chief," Snow said to Dane. "The man is in your section."

"It's just against regs, is all," Dane mumbled.

"This is not the English navy," Levere said. "It isn't even the American navy. Did you have to do that, chief?"

"I suppose I thought I must," Snow said. "Otherwise I would not."

Brace stood, nearly stumbled, looked amazed to find himself upright. He rubbed the red flush on his mouth and seemed to be counting his teeth. His eyes adjusted to his upright condition. His mouth pulled into a quavering line, and then his eyes reflected awe, or, it may be, understanding, but they certainly reflected one of the countless varieties of love. He walked in a tentative way through the office and to the open wardroom door. Knocked.

"You've been up to your white hat in troubles, sailor." Levere, normally remote and with full trust in his section leaders, and with a temper that was rare and thus awesome, did not like what he thought was about to happen.

"To speak to Chief Snow, sir." Brace stood erect, with outthrust and trembling lower jaw, as resolute-seeming (were it not for his green paint) as an advertisement for breakfast cereal. "I apologize," Brace said. "I deserved it."

"Indeed you did," Snow told him, "and the apology is accepted."

"Why do you apologize?" At close range Levere's face was always mildly shocking. Beneath the swarthy Frenchness, and under the flesh of the left cheek, a small and ulcerous growth caused one side of his face to seem swollen.

"Because I was wrong—sir."

"We know that, sailor. Do you understand why?"

Brace mumbled. It was only clear that he understood a compulsion of feeling, and was not, in his scarcely burnished cynicism, able to articulate his feeling.

"You are a crew member of this ship," Levere told him, "with rights as well as duties. Chief Snow is technically outside of regs. Do you want this logged?"

"No, captain." Brace turned to Dane, and Brace's face for an instant was covered with despair. Then he squared his shoulders again, took a shallow breath. "I know what you think, chief, but I've been trying. I really have been trying."

"Cows try," Dane told him. "When they plop in a field. Get turned-to on that paint."

Brace, shocked at being repulsed, his grand gesture lost in cow plop, began to slump away.

"Sailor."

"Captain?"

"I was going to transfer you after that display with the paint. Chief Dane insisted it would be a mistake."

Brace stood, unable to absorb a further jolt of information.

"I am now willing to admit that Chief Dane is probably correct. Dismissed." As Brace left, Levere turned to Snow. "Set your gang to work on the shoring, then come to my cabin."

"I am physically not a large man," Snow said instead. "Now that I am once provoked, I am sure that the crew has no further questions."

"In that case, go about your duties." Levere shook his head, mused as if dreaming. "I thought it was the Irish who were supposed to be lucky."

Abner's yeoman Wilson was impressed when Howard told the story. "Where did Levere find that one?"

"A small fishing village. A place called Liverpool."

"Get off my back. I can read a chart."

"He got busted up and concussed on a Limey can doing escort during the war. It scrambled his brains. They dropped him off here and he liked the place."

"Look for the woman," yeoman Wilson advised.

"I always do," Howard said. "World without end."

The gray chill was momentarily held in check because of the

incedent between Snow and Brace. For a while men gossipped, laughed, formed estimates of Snow that they could live with, while thinking little that was new about Brace. Cutter *Abner* struggled. By the time *Abner* had *Clara* in tow, returning to the disabled *Ezekiel*, the story turned from the main street of the crew's attention to a back alleyway of disregard. It was a small memory, to be fished from a man's ditty bag of tales at some future time, on some future messdeck, where youth might need advice.

As the tale moved into shadows, and *Abner*'s problems increased, so also increased a cold sense of unease, punctuated by bursts of exasperation because *Abner* was forced to go it alone.

"That could be us out there," Glass complained.

"The sea got up," yeoman Wilson told Howard. "It was seven hours to *Clara* and twenty coming back. The jury rig on their steering broke twice."

"We didn't hear you send for a long time."

"Those fishing skippers had this crazy idea."

Clara, outbound, was fully iced.

"They tried to transfer ice," Wilson said. "Our cap went along with it for awhile, but the sea kept working."

In a gray dawn, cutter *Abner* steamed slowly through mist, keeping visual and radar check on its three charges. *Clara* and *Ezekiel* wallowed together, fending off, their crews a bucket brigade passing ice above a gray, cold sea. The hard-pitching, smaller *Hester C.* was streamed to a sea anchor two miles distant.

"And that's when the guy on *Joan of Arc* got hit?"

"Who does the first aid on your ship?"

"Me."

"Me, too," Wilson said. "Me and our cook. We'd ought to have a corpsman."

On *Joan of Arc*, a rusting cable had snapped, tearing away most of a man's face.

"We steamed at them flank," Wilson said, "and they were

making knots toward us. It only took a couple hours. Couldn't get a seaplane."

"I've seen them put down on open ocean."

"Not that open ocean."

"He was one of those hysterial Spanish guys, and he moaned all the time," Wilson continued in the clear tones of misery. "He moaned for five days straight an' all you could do was clean him up. Sulfa and bandages and soup and keep his breathing clear, and a little morph. Bone stickin' out of his face."

Abner, receiving the injured fisherman, wheeled back and returned rapidly to its three radar targets.

"I was still holding that guy's hand," Wilson said, "so I didn't see what happened. Our radioman, Diamond, told me."

Through the mist, *Hester C.* was a pitching, black and gray dot on a gray sea. As *Abner* closed, Diamond picked up the 7 x 50s to check the lobsterman's trim. He gasped, put down the binoculars and picked up the 20-power telescope. The figure of a man was bending over the well of dead lobsters.

"I wish it swamped," yeoman Wilson said. "That guy fixed his old lady good. Nobody will ever buy that thing."

"Nobody was aboard."

"Sure there was," said yeoman Wilson, and his chalky face contorted with indignation and confusion. "Not when we got there, of course. He just zapped out like if you pulled the plug on a movie."

"But that was the end of it?"

"That was the end of the scary part," Wilson said. "We finally got all the tows rigged, and we started off at a red-hot two knots, and that's when things got miserable. That's when we started breaking towline."

68

VIII

〰〰〰〰〰〰〰〰〰〰〰〰〰〰〰〰〰〰〰〰〰〰〰〰

BRACE'S SHAVED head was a tribute to Amon's engaged concern, which was not patchy although Brace's haircut certainly was. In an attempt to save as much fur as possible, Amon snipped, clipped, razored, turned Brace's head this way and that, and proclaimed the finished job a masterpiece—and so it was, had Brace been a pagan living in Samoa. To the surprise of all hands, Brace took his ordeal with the insensateness of the Buddha. The mirror explained to him that he had a high forehead, above which, and fairly far aft, a low pool of fuzz rose like a spring, to flow forward in a questioning way toward his left ear where it was absorbed back into the water table of his skull an instant before it arrived. The right side of his head was clipped and spotted with patches of baldness, like an aging Marine suffering a twenty-year bout with jungle crud.

"It will grow back," Amon mourned. "Such is my fate."

Lamp, as practical as any cook ever gets, suggested that Amon borrow a camera and preserve the record. Amon sniffed with oriental disdain. "I am not a tourist," he told Lamp, then paused, " . . . although I am a very long way from home."

"You look like you got hit by a flight of seagulls," Glass told Brace. "Sue the Chinaman."

"Like bilge scraping," said Fallon.

"Like shark bait," said Conally.

"Your envy is ugly," Amon told them. "You would foul up a free lunch. You would despoil the Last Supper."

"You are a heathen—yes—heathen." Lamp slammed the door of the oven, turned. "Now look what you made me do."

Dane sniffed like a consumer inspecting popcorn at the concession in a seedy theatre. "I liked him better when he was painted," Dane said to Conally. To Brace he said, "Get up the mast."

"The view is tremendous," Conally told Brace.

Dane yelled at the bridge watch. "Secure the transmitter. Man aloft. Acknowledge."

"I got it off," . . . a distant yell.

Starting at the base of the mast and working upward, Brace chipped patches of rust, applied red lead to cleaned steel at the end of each day, climbed above the drying red lead on the next day, like a clam digger gradually following a tide. "If I start him at the top, he'll get dizzy and fall off," Conally explained to Howard.

Day followed day. Brace looked like a kite tangled among the wires of a telephone pole. He was perfectly situated to be the first man to see cutter *Abner*, bulked like a small, white and concentrated dot beside dark cliffs as it towed its string of refugees—but he was not the first. His attention was directed at placing an even coat of paint on the mast.

Lamp was the first to see *Abner*, or so in later years he claimed. "Boys, I be double-dog-damn," claiming one more minor miracle in that flat procession of days that saw *Adrian* hang against the pier impeccably dressed, like a partygoer waiting forever for an undispatched taxi.

Abner looked like a missionary lady leading derelicts to soup and prayer. *Ezekiel* rode high, directly astern on a shortened tow, its load of fish returned to the mindless Atlantic, that maw of gulls and basking sharks. Behind *Ezekiel, Clara* seemed to huddle frightened and scorched on the water; smoke and burn like a Puritan brand staining the house where rust already worked beneath blisters of paint. Alongside *Abner*, on snubbed tow, *Hester C.* made brief, impelled, black and gray dashes, like a rebellious child trying to escape the determined grasp of a pedestrian aunt.

The appearance of the tawdry group of collected wanderers stilled work in Portland harbor. Men laid tools aside, or stepped from the salesrooms of ship's chandlers, or came blinking from bars, coal yards, fish sheds. In sympathy, it seemed, with the instincts of Lamp, each man in harbor wanted to be able to say that he had "seen it." *Hester C.*, the star of the show, was set loose from *Abner*, its engine started, and a seaman guided it to the end of the pier where it would huddle like a small, dark demon flanked by the bows of *Adrian* and *Abner*.

Wide-hipped workboats moved like aging bankers with ambitions killed by the redundancy of profit. They splashed to *Ezekiel* and *Clara*, put lines aboard, chugged with bored avariciousness toward repair docks in Portland. In South Portland an ambulance appeared at the foot of the pier to receive the faceless Spaniard. Aboard *Adrian*, men stopped work, drifted to the main deck, spilled slowly and respectfully down the gangway, following Levere. In its entire battered history, *Abner* had never enjoyed so many line handlers in attendance on a pier.

"No need for it, chum, no need—its fuel allocations are cut—truth?—we're not cruising—is that true, cap—true—true?—yes—okay, but look at those guys—no need for it, chum—yes, but just *look* at those guys—"

Abner's fantail was like a stubby explosion of neglect. In no man's memory had there ever been Irish pennants, discarded chafing gear, tangled line piled, heaped, shoved aside on that fantail. The uncovered winch was skewed, no doubt in range of eventual repair, but enough tilted to alarm the heart. A gear locker sat dented, and paint on the heavy steel was indifferently shattered by an exploding line, while above the locker a floodlight dangled, broken from its base and wearing shards of the glass lens. The new towline lay in two unconnected mounds, like rubble.

Clearly they were in a bad way on *Abner*. The dago radioman Diamond, ordinarily as clean and efficient as an electronics tube, appeared at the rail where, while docking, he customarily had no business. He grumbled dispassionate instructions to line handlers. His black hair was lank and filled with grease, his shirt ripped, and a mixture of oil and soot scarred his face below a formerly white hat that seemed to have been dipped in the bilges.

A bosun's mate limped, leaned heavily against a stanchion like a man supported only by his conscience, while seamen stood stupidly at the rail, holding lines that they studied with the dull curiosity of idiots. *Abner*'s captain slumped on the wing, muttering helm and engine orders to yeoman Wilson, who stood inside at the telegraph and muttered to the helmsman. A quartermaster wandered aimlessly on the flying bridge, like a man trying to remember an errand.

Abner's crew, it developed, had been standing six on, two off, six on, two off, for over five days. Had the crew been able to sleep on those two-hour breaks, their job would have only been terribly difficult.

"It was just a nothing kind of sea," yeoman Wilson told yeoman Howard. "Maybe ten- to twelve-foot swells, but they were wide. No matter how you rigged, part of the tow would be hitting the backside of one just as you were coasting down the front of another. Line broke six times."

Yeoman Howard, recalling similar fiascos, although none so great, and with a resolution to do better by Lamp whom he had possibly in some way offended, took his feelings of indetermination to Lamp.

"The winch tore up on the first day when they tried to adjust the tow to that crazy sea. They walked the line the rest of the time. All hands."

"New towline . . . " Had Lamp been informed of God's suicide, his universe could hardly have been more shaken.

"They went through every scrap of line they had aboard," Howard said. "They had to pump *Clara* three times. *Ezekiel* was yelling about being in the middle of the tow, afraid it would spring the keel."

"It must of sprung the keel," said Lamp. "They wouldn't tow to a dry dock just for a busted engine."

"Helmsman on the lobster boat, helm watch, towing watch, steaming watch . . . the line broke a couple of the bosun's ribs."

"Lucky. He was lucky."

"He sure was." Howard, in spite of the warm galley, shivered.

"I been to the fantail," Lamp admitted, "to look at the new line. I got this queasy feeling, like."

One by one the men drifted aft to look at the new line.

"I forgot the date," Lamp said, less portentously than Howard expected. "It's gone and turned to September."

"Just keep something in the pot," Howard said. "Those guys are going to wake up starving."

The secular world of a ship rarely extends beyond its own gangway, and only under intimate conditions.

Brace, like a cloud-walker on the mast, looked down at the curious sight of *Adrian's* crew boarding *Abner*. *Abner's* crew disappeared to gamey-smelling and finally immobile bunks where they lay like a small company of mostly clothed corpses, drawn faces gradually relaxing beneath the red nightlights that were turned on in the waning afternoon. Howard, checking the crew list, stood silent, counting, hugely moved by a small intimation of fear.

On *Adrian*, the bosun Conally stood at the foot of the mast and yelled, "Secure the job."

Had they been offered, *Abner's* captain would not have accepted watchstanders from the Base, which was too remote, too uncertain. He would have asked his crew to muddle through. Levere, given the same circumstance, would have refused as well.

"Move quiet," Dane hissed above *Abner*'s fantail. "Flake the line on the pier. They'll want to repair it themselves."

Brace, knowing the spectacular solitude of the mast, and having had time to consider the largest implications of Snow's backhanding, stepped to earth with new convictions.

"I should be over there helping."

"We're splitting crew," Conally said. "Double watches. You take the four-to-mid."

"What can I do now?"

"Pretend we're steaming," Conally told him. "Sack out until your watch. Let your hair grow."

Once again, the gray chill moved down the pier, insinuating between the ships, concentrating at the end of the pier where *Hester C.* rode on its mooring, unclaimed, certainly unloved, and absolutely feared. By the time Brace relieved the watch at 1600, the local newspaper was on the streets carrying an ignorant, journalistic account, together with a ten-year-old photograph of *Abner*'s captain taken when he was exec on the snatcher *Bluebell*. Various deities, all of whom could be accused of inventing the sea, and of instigating the notion of things that float, were flagrantly thanked in Portland's missions and churches.

Brace relieved the watch, checked the phone, entered weather observations in the log, turned up the radio, looked to the mooring, and made himself acquainted with the current traffic in Portland harbor. As the dusk gathered, he surveyed the lights of Portland where, it might be, lonely young women of worth waited with hope for the friendship of some man who did not wear a white hat. As dusk accumulated, and the tide fell, *Hester C.* dropped below the end of the pier until only the mast was visible.

With Dane and Snow aboard *Abner*, Conally found himself serving as OD, and it was Conally, shaken from sleep sometime after 2300, who looked into the pale, terrified features of Brace, who, although not yet drooling, was idiot-eyed. Conally was on his feet and starting to dress before Brace could speak.

"It's adrift."

"What?"

"That lobster boat is adrift."

Conally relaxed. "Things drift," he said, preparing himself almost optimistically for an eventual return to sleep. "We'll call the Base. Let them pick it off with a small boat."

"Things don't drift against the tide," Brace chattered.

Hester C., like a small blot of self-destruction, faced the tide in a drift toward the mudflats.

Conally, shaken to the denied roots of his Indian-raised soul, swore later that his hair stood straight. He raced to the bridge, called the Base, watched a picket boat pick up the tow and return it to the pier. Conally checked the lines, found them sound, and made up the mooring himself.

"Sometimes the tide pools up," he told Brace. "It gets to working in circles." He checked his watch. "Time to call your relief."

Brace, withdrawn to silence, and with shame over his fear, returned to the bridge. Conally went belowdecks like a confused bear retreating to a cave—only to be wakened an hour and a half later by Glass, who was resolute and in control, and perfectly articulating a language that Conally thought was either Arabic or Armenian.

"Speak English."

"It's doing it again," Glass said.

IX

~~~~~~

SMALL CRAFT warnings on a clear day are like a bright exclamation. Beneath slanting sunlight, wind pebbles the water in small runs across the harbor, and the flag is a red tongue that wags, laughs, gossips about the sun, mountains, islands, and wind. Gulls fly straighter, their circles flatten, and they rise or descend on the wind like squawking and feathered yo-yos. Distant in the harbor, dories appear bobbing between splashes, while buoys ride solid, displaying the wind as they separate the lightly running chop. Susurrous murmurs wake between the hull and the pier, and men, not exactly intimidated by the cooling wind, place their hands on sunlit steel of the leeward side where there remains a memory of excellent warmth. The breeze nudges like a sniffing, snuffling dog, nose-bumping indifferent elbows, intent on gaining affection. Men step belowdecks to rifle seabags from which are fetched questionable-looking socks, watch caps, long johns and mittens that have survived the preceding winter. On the messdeck and in the crew's compartment, foul-weather gear is pulled almost apologetically into view. Needles are clumsily threaded and loose buttons tightened, with triangular snags patched and sealed with tar.

"Fit out," Glass advised Brace.

"Come payday."

"Come first liberty. I'll take you to the credit Greek. I rake off a percentage."

"So does the Greek," Howard said. "If you want the perfect crime, open an Army-Navy store."

"I already got the perfect crime," Glass told him. "After years of study. I'm going to design perfect crimes and sell them."

"For a percentage."

"For a flat fee *and* a percentage."

"It's warm in the engine room," Brace said, "and that's where I'm going."

"You're going to the Army-Navy store."

Brace, in single-minded determination, was, approximately, mentally unsound on the subject of the engine room. He was engrossed with a dream that had been sketchy before his days on the mast. Now, that dream was firmed into the maniac certainty that Levere, Dane and Snow would welcome what Brace's unbalanced mind called "logic." While other men walked the chilling decks, watched repair proceed on *Abner* and cast hesitant glances at the wayward and ugly *Hester C.*, Brace thought only of the engine room.

Hester C. settled into watchful sullenness that forced quartermaster-designate Rodgers, formalistic, Catholic-inclined, skinny, exact, red-haired, and plagued with ceremony, to make the sign of the cross each time he walked the gangway. Sometimes Rodgers crossed himself before saluting the colors, sometimes after. "I try to make it half and half," he confided to Lamp, " 'cause it's hard to say which should come first."

Lamp, believing that the pope was a kind of superannuated rabbi, opted for prayer without ceasing.

"You got to be kidding," Rodgers said. "Protocol. You ever hear of protocol, cook?"

"Something pulled that tramp to us," Lamp complained. "It wasn't protocol."

"It was *Abner*."

"You are simpleminded. Simple."

"I climbed all over that scow," Conally told them. "There's nothing different about that boat from any other boat."

"It's plotting mischief, boys, I got a feeling."

"Pull the plug," said Howard. "Poof."

"And have it lay at the end of the pier for always."

Gunner Majors, ordinarily quiet, as if stilled by his preoccupation with things that explode, claimed that *Hester C.* would make a wonderful target. The men stood before the galley, or loafed on the messdeck, their heads idle—except for the jaws—their hair still short but now untrimmed; red faces, wan faces, swarthy faces. About them lay clean decks, squared-away gear, and the encroaching idleness that was dulling and insensitive and blunt. The coffee urn steamed. Amon hummed, spoke to himself in Japanese as he scrubbed an immaculate wardroom.

Adrian seemed like a polished piece of antique crystal stored forever behind the closed doors of a buffet. The men hesitated, remained silent, as if finally captured by a grim decree that made them outcasts even from their avowed purpose. Then forward and distantly sounding through steel bulkheads, the blurred resonance of a bell arrived like an echo.

"Calling the engine room."

"It's another drill."

"I told you I had a feeling, boys."

"Something's up."

"We're starting to get some breeze."

Gale warnings, which almost never occur on a clear day, are like a dark and hollering mouth of triumph. The sky lowers in the northeast, and against the footings of the million-dollar bridge, gray foam rises like the fingers of the harbor. Yachts, swinging at anchor, seem the focus of attack by fleets of dories as owners hastily arrive, secure sail and loose gear, chug engines into life and move out in search of moorage. Toward the Portland Head, the sea, graying toward the sky, begins to pile and churn, white-maned with the wind; and the dark green islands lie like black smears fronted and circled by rocks that carry surf in their teeth. On the windward side of the pier, *Abner* is flung in short thumps by crashing water, and to leeward *Adrian* tugs at its lines, falls backward into the small resulting trough, is surrounded by the rush and sigh and hasten of swift water. At the Base the new signal, twin flags, reports in sharp snaps from the tower, while across the bristling, whitening harbor, above the blown spray, a thin layer of black rises in churning dust from the coal yards to march like a line drawn across the windy face of Portland.

"Plane down."

"He's bought it."

"Three planes. Air Force."

"Get off my back."

"I think it's three. That's what James yelled at Dane."

"I'd like to yell at Dane. Chum, if I ever yell at Dane."

"You'll yell, 'yessir chief, yep', that's what you'll yell."

"How can three planes go down at once?"

"Out of the way, there. Quit tryin' to explain the Air Force."

Engines rumble onto the line, dark smoke like a period to an idle sentence pops from the stack and into the wind. The engines settle, the smoke disappears. Yeoman Howard tumbles down the gangway in a splayed run, bumps against the wind like a comma, his watch cap battening his ears, the wind at his face while he crosses to *Abner* where yeoman Wilson dashes along the main deck to the gangway.

"You, too."

"Six guys out there."

"Give me that." Wilson grabs sailing lists and mail, runs to drop them at the Base. Aboard *Adrian*, seamen single up on the mooring while Dane stands on the wing with the broad certainty of a tugboat, bellowing. About the decks Conally secures gear, rages. The gangway is shoved clattering toward Howard, to be pulled by him past the lip of the pier. He swings aboard forward of the breast line, turns to see Wilson dashing from the Base in jerky bursts against the wind. On the bridge the high-tuned crackle of the radio, faint in the wind, blanks as James sends the departure message, "Various courses and speeds, maneuvering to assist"; the lines let go, tended by Glass, who leaps aboard as if propelled by the wind; and *Adrian*, on cold engines, moves slowly into the stream to gather speed evenly as combustion raises engine heat.

"Nine minutes. Log it. Zero nine fifty-two."

"What took so long?"

"The cook was talkin'."

Maligned Lamp, appearing on the main deck, watches *Adrian*'s stern slide past the dark, ugly blot of *Hester C.* He shakes his head, retreats below to secure the galley as *Abner* noses from the pier. Decks of both ships seem momentarily peopled with men making up and securing lines. In the channel, *Adrian* brushes at the heavy chop, presses, vibrates from engines, from shaft; a vibration sensed more than felt, like a football lineman poised instantly, a split second ahead of the count, delicately timed to avoid a penalty. Men off watch, hesitant with the anxiety of a job that offers no current action, drift to the messdeck to wait for news brought by radioman James who drops galleyward like a pale Lord, his coffee mug dangling from one thin hand like a small and forgotten chalice.

"The word. What's the word?"

Amon, headed forward with coffee for the bridge gang, pauses, listens. Three trainers are out of fuel and down.

"That kind without propellers," said McClean. "I don't trust nothing without a propeller."

Amon pauses, then begins his climb to the main deck. "Jets would splash hard in this weather."

"In any weather."

"Headed up to Bangor?"

"Along that line."

"We won't find 'em."

"We'll take a turn on trying."

On the occasion of his first visit to water above the shelf, Brace stood as stalwart as a young hound. He listened, seemed thoughtful, then went above to the main deck where he leaned on the rail as if fixed by romance as strong as McClean's faith in things that churned. The luminous and beckoning engine room, the lost Mona, the harsh words and rage of Dane were doubtless lost in the gray mist and blown spray rising before the lighthouse at Portland Head which for more than a century and a half had stood watch over curious sights and cold survivors of the sea.

Howard, who in lucid moments swore to Lamp that all prayer was directed to the ridiculous, approached.

"You'll love it in a little while," he said to Brace. "Wait until we clear the head."

Brace turned with the vacuous look of total absorption in great matters. He seemed surprised by the intrusion of another consciousness into his arena of sensation. His watch cap fell to his eyebrows, from beneath which his eyes were dark brown and lightly glazed with either romance or memory, or possibly wind. He steadied himself, leaned against the rail, both hands forward and gripping easily like a magician or a strong man who was singly holding together the ancient collection of parts that was the cutter *Adrian*.

"I like it," he said. "I've been thinking how much this don't look like Illinois."

Howard, who in a dim way may have sensed a bond between himself and Brace in some near past, paused, then resumed his task.

"You learn the helm, then practice steaming. Twelve-to-two on the bridge, two-to-four in the engine room." Then, a man pressed into confidences by the rare occasion of privacy, he said, "It isn't like Ohio, either."

"You're from Ohio?"

"Did you think you invented it?"

The glaze over Brace's eyes disappeared in favor of intuition and recognition. He pushed himself upright from the rail, looked at Howard.

"I guess I thought I did. Does everybody?"

"I don't know, but probably I'll think about it."

Beyond the Portland Head, the sea rises unfettered in its crush toward the land. Above the widely moving swell which lifts and drops vessels as surely as the faith asked of a philosophic premise, runs a chopping swell that is a creature born of wind. The confused sea delivers shocks against the hulls of the largest ships, and smaller vessels nose the wind like determined and uneasy immigrants to a sometimes violent land. The wind, flavored with salt, picks spray from the bow, to wash decks, house, rails, the unused and unthought-of guns; wind rising from the tops of waves to swirl spume like a dust devil awhirl across a plain. Salt accumulates in the corners of men's mouths, to be licked away, causing a momentary taste of the sea's huge proclamation. The wind speaks in the open tones of unmuted instruments. Gales do not howl or scream or screech, as does a storm. They moan, weep, play the blues, are lubricating and liquid over lonesome, tricky waters.

"It's a tough rap," Glass said to Brace. "Some say to puke and get it over with. Others say that if you once start pukin' you can't get stopped."

Brace, making a choice, or more likely in the firm grasp of his body's knowledge, spilled breakfast to leeward in illustration of young wisdom. Then he climbed weak-kneed and pale to the bridge and began to discover some of the things that a helm will not accomplish.

After the first urge of action and compassion, *Adrian*'s crew settled into the routine of a steaming watch that pointed the vessel toward unknown positions and easily guessed agony. In September in Maine, and with a little fat, a lot of thrashing, and all the luck left to him, a man can sometimes live for twenty minutes in the water. If the crews of the planes had not made it to their life rafts, their books were already closed. If they were on the rafts, jacketed and booted, their paltry scrap of canvas clutched over them against the wind, hypothermia might not spin them from the edge of their circle for fifteen or twenty hours.

On small ships, as watch follows watch, and as the sea continues through shocks to search for loose gear, and, finding none, seeks to loosen gear to fling it, daily work on the ship ceases. Men who are not yet reduced to walking on bulkheads are still unable to trust their tools, their sustained balance, even their intent.

Amon, who suffers in the first hours of large movement, lies huddled beneath a table of the messdeck in Asiatic contemplation, from which, like Lazarus, he will in a few hours rise wide-eyed and knowledgeable from the explored depths of a great mystery.

"If he'd just quit fighting it and puke, he'd be all right. I keep telling him." Lamp, who is smart about the galley in his heavy-shanked way, builds, constructs, fusses over half-filled vats of soup and regiments of sandwiches, the most that can be claimed from this kind of sea.

Men off watch sit on the messdeck, or sack out in jerkily plunging bunks. The Indian Conally roams the slick upper decks in communion with wind and water, ostensibly checking against things adrift that may crash or vanish. Heat swirls through the grates of the fiddley, where Howard, in time, passing forward to the bridge, sniffs, as if he expects sulphur to rise from the hot depths in which Snow, like a small brown bird, perches beside the engine-order-telegraph and before the great bank of dully gleaming gauges, dials and valves that look like waving, plunging sculpture.

Howard stands arrested, silenced, emptied, in foreboding, in heart-shocking horror; watching a stance he has seen so often in excursions across this fiddley—the wide-legged, hunch-shouldered concentration of the drowned Cecil Jensen standing on oily plates beside the port engine; a wiping rag dangling from a hip pocket, another rag dangling from one hand. The stance is a collection of tallness compacted to bulk, only a little less unique than a thumbprint.

Howard shudders, reduces a yell, a scream, back into his instinctive interior, and stands in dispraise of his eyes which have fooled him.

It is only Brace standing there, timid, alert, entranced among the heavy voices of the engines.

On the bridge, Dane stands like a brick mortared between loran and radio. He looks seaward, squinty-eyed and thin-mouthed, unimpressed by the hook of Rodgers's body that dangles headless from the rubber mask over the radar scope. Glass twirls the helm to meet the sea, twirls back, the gyro repeater dances, swings. Levere mutters over the plot. James fiddles with log sheets, waits.

"How's the set?"

"Sea return, cap. We could miss a freight train." Rodgers backs from the radar mask, blinking, a man reconnected.

"Eyes, chief. Call watchstanders."

The radio pops, blanks.

"*Abner* calling."

"We'll take the seaward leg."

The ships drop their mutual course; *Abner* climbs the chart to the northwest while *Adrian*, advancing under the spinning, kicky helm in the hands of the watchful Glass, beats to the southeast.

X

~~~~~~

WATCHES CHANGED, darkness approached, and the gray sea turned black, marked by luminous and crashing runs of opalescent foam. Men carrying binoculars moved from the wings to the flying bridge, thrust into a netherland of increasing wind, and separated from the interfering, dull red lights below. *Adrian* paced back and forth across sixty-nine degrees latitude in a search across a line. Phosphoresence spun from the bow. The muted stack rumbled, whispered. As temperatures skidded, lookouts on watch wrapped mufflers across their mouths, turned from a defensive oblique that put the wind most often on their covered ears and raw cheeks, facing with greater frequency into the wind so that their breath would not fog the glasses. Each man searched his sector, silent, occasionally stomping feet against the deck and listening to the deepening tone and quality of the wind which worked across the vibrating strings of the halyards.

"Report everything," Conally instructed Brace.

"You can't see anything."

"Them rafts are yellow," Conally said. "Water will be washing around them. Sometimes they have flares."

"The trouble is, I think I see something and then it goes away."

"Don't stare. Look to one side. Look away, then look back."

"Why don't they all have flares?"

"They all do. Guys get scared and use them up. They get too cold and drop them."

Brace, as if chewing the information, stood hunched into an old foul-weather jacket that was in need of overhaul. "Planes have been flying over all day."

"Planes . . . couldn't spot a whale on a dinner plate."

On the bridge, Dane hunkered before the radar mask, he, too, now seemingly headless, thus less bulky, almost thin. He was less threatening as his face appeared to begin and end between flared nose and chin. Bosun striker Joyce, haggard not from fatigue but from proximity to Dane, spun the helm to meet a sea, spun it back. Levere, captain, who had been on the bridge for twelve hours and who would remain until the flyers were a clear fatality, slouched in a tall bridge chair. As the hours passed, and as Levere's experience combined with intuition in his communion with wind and water, the westward leg lengthened.

No one (nor would any have dared ask) knew how Levere—trusted at the time, and trusted without question afterward—managed his conscience over the drowning of Jensen. If Levere was of the cynical French, he was also of New England, and he was the captain. In that past winter of piling seas that saw Jensen under, Levere remained as remote from the crew as ever. After Jensen's death, exhausted men saw that Levere was increasingly reluctant to break off any search. He stayed on the grounds, mutely answering the cold and killing sea, or answering his conscience. *Adrian*'s crew took a more reasonable view, holding that Jensen had tugged his final problem into his own spaces, and then slammed the hatch.

86

Yeoman Howard, who in Lamp's opinion "made too much of things," thought long and carefully about the matter. Howard had a special advantage. His occupation made him resemble a knitting needle. While Amon was a constantly running thread tying galley to messdeck to wardroom, Howard's job forced him into a skein of movement that covered the ship. In his busy way he was obnoxious, like a thin-minded bureaucrat, declaiming under law the divine right to distribute the largess of misery tendered by a loving government.

If, as Howard was often forced to point out, he must show Levere a constant watch list of the least tired men, that did not mean that he enjoyed it. He was scrupulous in scheduling his own watchstanding—the single reason why a sometimes driven crew managed to put up with him at all.

After Jensen's death, Howard muttered privately to Conally that the old man was taking it hard. Levere was prone to inactivity and silence.

"Like he's brooding," Howard told Conally.

"What's to brood about? We done our best."

"That's not the point."

Now, in another season, the point began to reassert itself.

Your large ship, suffering a thirty degree roll, finds the matter so monstrous that the event is entered in the log. *Adrian* (and electrician Wysczknowski swore this each time the rolling ship tripped his generator off the line) would toss its heart out on a duck pond. As the night drifted slowly past in spume, sharp shocks and breaking waves, the constant battering combined with the fact of too few watchstanders. Fatigue common to a night sweep at sea descended. Watches changed, then changed again, then changed again. The gale faltered, renewed, seemed trying to decide whether to tuck it in, or change over and become a full storm. In heavy, blanketing dark that was penetrated by the thin skim of a wary-seeming dawn, Lamp shushed and cautioned and troubled over Amon's health.

"I don't know why you don't just puke."

"Buddhists don't," Amon said, "or me, either. It's no cinch to be Hawaiian."

Howard trudged away from watch on the flying bridge. He descended a ladder to the main deck, entered through a hatch, crossed the fiddley in a mild stupor, glancing below for portents and finding none. Wysczknowski now sat at the board. Masters, a tall snipe who had a face that looked like an elf's, stood gazing at machinery, bracing himself against a rail, muttering; in elvish, perhaps.

Howard crossed the fiddley, trudged to the messdeck. He drew watchstander coffee from a small pot as Amon prepared the large coffee urn. Howard stared at the steaming mug of coffee as if debating whether to drink the stuff or use it to warm his hands. He hesitated again, between the alternatives of sleep or a wait for boiled eggs and toast from Lamp's sloshing, rattling machinery.

"*Abner's* broken off the search," he said. "Those guys have been down for twenty-two hours."

"We've lost 'em." Lamp's voice was filled with honest misery.

"Secure it soon. Head back in." Amon poured a brown stream of ground coffee, watched the roll of *Adrian* tip his hand to throw a dry sprinkle of brown across the messdeck. "I always spill. I tell myself I won't. I tell myself, Amon, this time . . . but look at it, how clever."

"You sound like Glass."

"I know a great deal about life."

" 'Tis bad luck, losing the first ones of the year."

"I don't think we'll break off," said Howard. "I think the old man will hang around until District sends us in."

"To our misery."

"You're not in the water, sonny. Don't talk about misery—"

"Hold up . . . we're coming around."

"A contact? Maybe a contact?"

Adrian heeled from a westward leg and drove southeast,

slipping sideways in a quartering sea as it made a dash farther down the line of search. At full speed the ship bucked, kicked, lunged in heavy forefoot stomps to starboard, the mast like a great crucifix attempting to dip the waves as if to calm them.

"Cap knows we'll get called in," radioman James told a few men assembled on the messdeck. "He's trying to steal a little sea room."

"He's tough. Ol' cap is tough." The mulatto McClean wore an ambitious black patch of grease on his dull-skinned cheek. "Lift eggs from under a settin' hen."

"Lift eggs right off your plate if this sea keeps up."

Farther south, in the gleaming District offices, sleek and chubby yeomen, radiomen, and bored JOODs no doubt finished morning coffee, licked donut sugar from plump, shore-going fingers, and noticed that *Adrian* had not yet broken off. By the time the message to secure arrived, Levere had stolen sixteen miles. *Adrian* set a homeward course, zigzagging across a westward line and inshore from its former line of search. The morning routine set in as jolts and spray climbed high about the decks from the northeast leg while cold men dropped like slick, wet stones down the ladder to the messdeck. The men were vaguely angry with the sea.

"What good does this do?"

"Levere's still giving it a shake."

"He's giving *us* a shake."

Gunner Majors brushed spray from his eyebrows as he kept his glasses tipped away from wind that scoured the flying bridge. No gulls flew on such a day, no basking sharks lay aslumber on the sea, and while flotsam was likely within fifty miles of the coast, Majors would later say that he already knew he had a target. He lifted the glasses to confirm. Dropped them to hang from one hand. Took a deep breath and lifted them to reconfirm. He leaned forward to press a buzzer beside a voice tube.

On the westward, inshore leg, sea anchor unstreamed, like a

yellow mite on the gray immensity of water, the raft appeared, disappeared, appeared, tossed sporadic and water-filled, unbailed, like the last beat of a dying heart.

"All hands. All hands."

In the engine room, bells clanged and the pulse of engines broke free from its metronome throb. Forward in the crew's compartment, sleeping men felt the thrust of the engines. They tossed in their sacks, fumbled with belts buckles looped from waists around the rails of bunks. They slid blinking onto the rising and unsteady deck, rebuckling belts with one hand, reaching for foul-weather gear with the other while they braced against the thrust of *Adrian* by jamming butts between bunks or against angles formed by lockers. In the engine room, Snow appeared like a short puff of magic, while above his head on the grates of the fiddley, men's feet hammered, staggered, bore pairs of hands toward the boat deck and the main deck. On the starboard wing a hatch erupted against the wind, as Dane, hollering with the certainty of an epistle, stubby as a boulder, yelled to the boat crew. Chappel relieved the helm and *Adrian* pressed in a sweep that would take it around the raft and place the bow into the sea. James wrote the log, danced thinly as he reached for radio message blanks and began to scrawl the contact report. Howard headed aft across the boat deck and down the ladder to the fantail to unlash steel basket stretchers. Above them all, Majors stood on the flying bridge, remote, his glasses sweeping the horizon, that vast orphanage.

Brace, the newest wanderer over water, stood beside Conally on the boat deck as Conally stripped the canvas cover off the boat. "Stand down to the main deck," Conally told him. "Make way for the boat crew."

"What'll I do?"

"Stop being stupid. Man the rail to fend off."

Dane, Conally, Glass, Joyce and Rodgers jumped, sat beside shipped oars, riding the boat in the wind of the deck like men preparing for a sail across the sky. Fallon, McClean and Racca tended lines, fended off, and the boat dropped in rapid jerks toward the sea, a controlled crash.

"Unhooked forward."

"Unhooked aft."

"Oars. Get 'em over. Dig."

Howard staggered forward, packing a bulky stretcher, the straps free and dangling like a machine of the Inquisition prepared to clasp a victim. He bumped into Brace.

"What? What?"

"Stand by to take their lines. Unhook those chains. Let down fenders."

McClean arrived. "Child," he said to Brace, "do it this-a-way." To Howard he said, "I got it."

"Blankets," said Howard vaguely, and dashed toward a hatch beyond which brooded the medical locker.

Dane stood at the sweep, grunted orders, swore thin-mouthed and violent as the boat returned, sliding into the lee made when Levere turned the ship. Dane's mouth hammered out shapes of words above his eyes which flashed with eternal-seeming pain; either the hot pain of rheumatism or the cold burn of the sea. In the boat a flyer bent forward, jammed between two oarsmen, leaning like a drunk or a propped dead man against the post of Conally's back, while Conally dabbed at the sea with an oar, ineffective, off balance.

With the helm trusted to the hands of his first quartermaster, Levere appeared on the main deck as the boat came alongside.

"How is he, chief?"

"Near froze."

"Can he talk?"

"He's too froze."

"The other one?"

"Not a chance."

"Chief Snow to the messdeck," Levere told Brace. "On the double, sailor." Levere turned to Howard. "Assist Chief Snow. Get this man talking."

"Easy there, take it easy."

With no time to brood over his summary relief from a job he detested in the first place, Howard helped swing the stretcher aboard. The flyer was pale, vaguely blue, as though a spectral self rose from beneath his flesh. Wet clothing bunched on either side of the compressing straps, and drops squeezed from the fabric to run across a sheen of deep water that lay like a well of cold in his waterproofs. His legs were held by the straps, but his feet were free to flop with the movement of the ship. He was without control of his lower body, and his puffy eyelids were red with cold and salt. His lips trembled, opened, closed, opened, smiled. The man seemed amused at the cleverness of a satisfactory speech, just delivered from tombs and cast wisely before an ignorant but temporarily interested world. His short hair glistened with water, his fingers clutched.

At the head of the stretcher, and with McClean at the foot, Howard staggered toward the after hatch and the ladder to the messdeck. Dane cursed from his position alongside the ship. Men grunted. The small boat turned away from *Adrian* and headed back for the raft, where the second pilot lay sloshing in unbailed water. Chief Snow flitted from fiddley to passageway to the ladder leading to the messdeck.

At the head of the ladder Howard turned, took a new grip on the stretcher and braced himself against a bulkhead to regain balance before making a backward descent. He glanced through the hatch leading to the fiddley, that fiddley where Howard had recently been shocked because he thought he had seen Jensen.

Now Amon stood on the grates, staring downward into the engine room; rigid, fixed, Amon's open mouth trying to search for any sound as he stood frozen in wide-eyed horror.

XI

~~~~~~

IN THE red-inked business of mercy at sea, a corpse represents failure. Cold eyes stare or are backwardly rolled, white. That flat and toneless stare causes among seamen a pinching sense of harm, of futility. The pinch is as sharp as ice behind your ear. Men feel nebulous guilt and small grief. Corpses are partners to huge but repressed fear. The fear is diamond-backed and sharklike. Corpses are rolled in canvas and stored on the fantail. They are bulky and awkward to wrap. Stiff limbs are rigidly fixed in a hundred antic shapes, the slate gone blank in its arrested scamper, the world dissolved into time that will forgive the most harlequin mimicry. Most fresh corpses exude some blood, and you can predict that the blood will be watery and weak. Stale corpses gush with other secrets. Mouths are always open and newly washed. Jaws dangle, surrounding raw tongues with a small circus ring of teeth. The jaws are not artless. They have spoken final words from a great gulf emptied of all but one fact.

Men carry a corpse to the fantail. They secure it, either by rough handling and slightly restrained violence, or else with a tenderness that its owner could hardly have been lucky enough to know when the thing was still alive. Then the men turn back to the messdeck, or stand in the hatch of the galley, or droop on the fiddley to stare, themselves corpselike, into any source of heat. If the corpse was once male, as the great majority are, conversation will eventually open on the messdeck with a giggle. A man will recall a shore-going episode. The talk will be of women.

"Bad luck," whispered Lamp. "We don't get more than three or four deaders a year, and now we're starting off with one."

"Keep it shut, cook. That guy is coming around."

Men avoid the fantail, and, if pressed in that direction by some duty, move quickly, with precision, and with short glances at the humped canvas. Every crew has at least one man who is fascinated, sometimes perverse; or with guilt and fear mixtured in such quantity that he is brought compelled to the boat deck to stand and stare aft, muttering, sometimes drooling.

"Snow had more experience. I maybe wouldn't have saved the guy." Yeoman Howard spoke to *Abner's* yeoman Wilson when *Adrian* once more swung against the pier. The rescued flyer was by then removed to an ambulance; the dead man lay enclosed in the back of a paddy wagon, his arms still grasping after his last enemy. On *Adrian's* fantail, Racca, obsessed, leaned on a hose as he flushed the deck. The straight-stream nozzle rose against his braced arms like a living creature struggling to snap away—a creature that could become high-bending, a tall snake arching and cracking and wielding sharp and deadly blows.

"We got the guy talking," Howard said. "His plane dunked first. That meant that the others were somewhere up ahead."

"We figured we might go back out," Wilson said.

"We found another raft. Upside down." Howard seemed to

94

be still looking, staring, absorbing the fact of a bouyant, bouncing, yellow raft, high-riding with futility. "Those were brand new planes. Fitted out with the wrong fuel gauges."

"So who do you kill?" Wilson's huge, chalky face seemed dispassionate as he gazed across the pier at Racca who directed the shattering water that knocked salt and the invisible traces of the dead from the decks. Then Wilson seemed to remember whom he was with. He looked at Howard, and he was helpless, angry, momentarily passionate. "So who do you kill, who?" He dropped his eyes, muttered. "I don't know why we put up with this, don't know."

"It was a carnival," Howard told him. "Amon was like a fruit salad. The new guy was ready to fight. Snow was working on that man in a way that I'd have been embarassed."

"Snow talks funny. That guy talks funny." Wilson was un-comfortable. He looked as though he feared that a deadly but familiar beast was about to come woofing from a cave.

"I don't mean that," Howard said. "There wasn't anything like that."

"Planes with bad fuel gauges."

"I was rubbing the guy's legs," Howard said. "Snow was putting on hot packs and rubbing his back and belly and crotch arteries."

"I guess you got to."

"That Snow just kept whispering." Howard spoke in a low voice, as though he still heard Snow's whispers, still stood beside Snow as they worked on the flyer; still attempted to sense meaning from Snow's broken, husky whispering, and the small, busy hands that moved with the certainty of a pump as the flyer's circulation was restored. "He just kept whispering, 'torpedoes, torpedoes, torpedoes,' just over and over."

"He got blowed up once. He was just scared."

"No," Howard said. "I don't understand everything I saw, but Snow wasn't scared."

"He only loves torpedoes."

Howard, almost wordless before the suspicious fact of near revelation, seemed resigned to the uselessness of speech. "I'm glad I missed that war."

"Stick around for the next one, chum. We can't have you being glad." Wilson paused, thought about it. "In the next one," he said, "try not to trust anybody's gauge but your own."

Across the pier, on *Adrian*'s boat deck, Conally appeared from behind the house. He was followed by Brace. Conally began unfolding the boat cover while Brace stood like a lank shadow as he waited to accept instruction on cleaning and securing and making ready the boat.

"Your boy looks okay now," Wilson said.

"No, he doesn't. You'd have to know him." Howard flipped vaguely through the small package of mail collected for him by Wilson. He looked at Wilson, as if they were about to share a secret, and then changed his mind. "He's kind of jammed up, is all." Then Howard changed his mind again. "We've got a mess going with that kid. It started just after we picked up the first guy."

The small boat, lap straked and carrying on its bows the placid information that it belonged to cutter *Adrian*, had seemed like a minor revolutionary battering at the gates of the gray, patriarchal sea. The boat was a small white smear on the water, and it seemed as uncertainly fixed as was Brace on his first search and rescue.

"He was actually doing pretty good," Howard told Wilson. "He was making mistakes, but he was willing."

Brace had hovered close beside Howard, standing at *Adrian*'s rail as they watched the boat which rocked, plunged, took spray and seemed for a moment to join with the yellow raft. Across a hundred yards of tossing water, Dane's voice was thin with propelling curses, as if only a voice of arrogance and scorn could answer the indifference of the heat-draining sea. *Adrian* came ahead slowly. Levere settled on the right measure of revolutions per minute. *Adrian* met the swell, treading like a dancer moving from quick, dramatic action into a slow coda. The small-boat's crew shipped oars. The sky was a gray, luminous frame suggesting that the sun had not yet abandoned the planet. Cold wind moved from the mouth of the luminosity like a dissenting opinion from a court of natural law.

"That's when we got that guy aboard," Howard told Wilson. "The old man wanted Snow fetched to the messdeck. He sent the kid."

Brace seemed to have a nesting instinct for the engine room. He had moved like a homing pigeon flying in heavy wind. *Adrian* was by then cross seas, wallowing, brought about by Chappel to make a lee. Men advanced about the decks in short rushes, were brought up against bulkheads or rails with jarring shocks. In the galley, a mug or bowl spun from the rubber fingers of a rack that was guaranteed to prevent all minor disasters. The crash was like the report of a small rifle echoing through open hatches and accompanied by the shout of Lamp's despair. Brace climbed the deck, clambered, advanced in small dashes, arrived at the engine room ladder. He descended and spoke to his hero, Snow.

"Take the board," Snow said to the elflike Masters. He turned back to Brace. "Back him up on the plates until I send relief." Snow disappeared up the ladder, and Brace, asked for the first time to be competent in a situation that was not a drill, stood watchful and prepared beside the port engine. He dangled a wiping rag from one hand and watched the brilliantly lighted engine room rise, dash sideways, fall, as *Adrian* slipped into the trough and seemed trying to shake the heavy engines loose from mountings or drive them through the hull. Lights flickered, flared in brilliant surges as the generator faltered and then took hold.

Brace had little training, but, for the moment, he had

enough. He listened for disturbance in the systems, studied what he knew of the fluid movement through piping. He was entranced, and might temporarily have forgotten his latest problem.

"Talked to Snow while they were on watch," Howard told Wilson. "Maybe that's why he blew up later."

"No transfer, huh?"

"Not until he hacks the deck. Not until Dane calls him a seaman."

"I understand your boy. Hate my own rate. I rather almost be a cook, even."

"You aren't nosy enough. Not even for a yeoman. But I know what you mean."

"He can make seaman in another six months."

"If the offer still stands," Howard said uncomfortably. "It was made before the steward went crazy."

Amon, his seasickness overcome, had trotted forward like a short shadow to the bridge with a half-filled pitcher of fresh coffee. He staggered and pinged and ponged in the passageway as *Adrian* rolled. The stretcher crew came through the hatchway, maneuvering the rescued flyer, and Amon gave way and stepped onto the fiddley. He began to cross the fiddley on a journey he had made a thousand unremarkable times. He glanced down into the flaring and flickering lights, was held fixed by the ghastly sight of Jensen standing on the plates. Amon opened his mouth to scream, found himself without breath or voice; or found himself under the slapping control of the satisfied and smiling Buddha. The stretcher party passed. Amon stood trembling. He conversed with his feet. He praised his feet. He lied to them with astounding deceptions in an effort to get them to walk. The hump-shouldered figure of Jensen stumbled against the roll of the ship. It righted itself like a clumsy doll. Amon stared. Stared. A wiping rag dangled from Jensen's hand, as it had always dangled from Jensen's hand when Amon had made trips across this fiddley. Jensen was sanely in control in this sea world, and because of that, Amon's world changed into a surreal and desperate place. The ship skidded, fell away, banged into the trough and the lights flickered, died, returned and then died again as the generator kicked off the line. Yells from below rose, jumped, swarmed in the darkness. Amon, deranged, heard Jensen's voice. In the distance, but rapidly approaching, moved the voice of Wysczknowski cursing loudly at the sea.

Amon's deceived feet began to slowly move him backward. He stepped from the fiddley into the after passage, turned, and slowly walked through a hatchway to the main deck. *Adrian* rolled, slammed, plummeted. Amon dumped the coffee into the scuppers. Then, softly treading the banging ladder, he took the pitcher to the galley, groping, and secured it with great care. Wordless, Amon walked to the wardroom past the grunting urgency of men who stripped the flyer and assisted Snow. Amon knelt on all fours and crawled beneath the wardroom table. When Lamp, abustle in official alarm, found him there an hour later, Amon was mute. He tried to speak. Produced a whimper.

Watches changed. On the flying bridge, Conally and Glass stood searching their sectors like men digging for one bright coin in that huge pocket of sea. They were remote, isolated, unreported. In Boston, Natchez, London, Madrid, Hong Kong, there occurred murders. Along the Yangtze there were murders, and in Moscow and in Lima, Peru. Somewhere in the east, murder occurred along a vaguely theoretical line termed MLR by Marines. Murder was like a wilted flower in Chicago and Rome. There was murder in L.A. and in Anchorage, in Frisco, Mexico City and Tampa. Conally and Glass searched, kept tight lips closed over teeth that, exposed, would ache in the wind. Glass sighted the second yellow raft. Conally saw that it was upside down.

"Still crazy?"

"He came out of it in three or four hours," Howard told Wilson, "then he went back in."

Murder ran red and surging in Tokyo and Buenos Aires, and it pulsed redly in Cape Town. Murder attended a fish war in Bristol Bay. Murder colored a street in Melbourne, popped like a small and hotly glowing flare in Sydney, in Paris, and Krakow.

"It got toward sunset," Howard told Wilson. "Lamp kidded Amon along. Got him talking. We put the flyer in the wardroom, and Amon was kind of hiding on the messdeck."

Brace, perhaps with curiosity over a rumored madman, or more likely in need of coffee after a turn on the flying bridge, descended to the messdeck. *Adrian* was corkscrewing on a downward leg that had the sea on its quarter. Brace carried a wet foul-weather jacket poxed with small, triangular tears. He had somewhere borrowed a needle and thread. In the bright lights of the messdeck his face no longer seemed unremarkable. His high forehead rising toward his brief cap of fur was damp from spray, and from sweat caused by hood and watch cap. His forehead wrinkled. His mouth, formerly lax and unimportant, was clamped in a knowledgeable line. In spite of the odds, he looked like a man who knew what he was doing.

Mother Lamp hovered about Amon. He clucked, joked, looked like a man fighting a chill. The brightly lit messdeck was damp and disarranged. A sprinkle of wet salt lay like a small white trail blazed across a table. The flyer's wet clothing hung drying in the galley, swinging with the plunge of the ship like a hanged man dancing. Lamp tsked. Amon murmured. Wysczknowski, his long Polack face, thin-nosed and blue-eyed beneath washed blond hair, slumped at the engineer's table. He fumbled a deck of moist, nearly undealable cards like a man who has newly discovered that he detests solitaire.

Amon looked up, round faced and open eyed. He licked a corner of his mouth, stuttered. He lifted one arm, placed a finger in his mouth as though trying to dislodge an elephant. He shuddered, gurgled, and went catatonic, pitching forward to the deck where he lay like a man fallen from a tall building. Lamp yelled, shrieked, shrieked, jumped upright as if pierced by a sharp iron weapon. Howard leapt from his retreat in the cubicle of the office, and Wysczknowski, as though thankful, tucked the pack of cards in his shirt pocket. Amon's eyes rolled back, the rigidity of catatonia disappeared and Amon's left arm thumped, flailed. His legs kicked. His body heaved and shuddered and flopped.

"Clear his tongue. Get a spoon. Don't put your hand in there."

"He's having fits."

"I think he's having epilepsy. A guy at the Base had it once."

Brace ran toward the galley, was caught by an original movement from *Adrian*, banged his shoulder on the coffee urn. He regained his balance, achieved the galley, and returned with a long wooden spoon. He passed it to Howard, then dropped to his knees in an effort to grab Amon's kicking, drumming legs. "Hold his head," Howard told Wysczknowski. "Don't let him kick you," he said to Brace. "This kid is stronger than he looks."

Lamp stood like a drooping distress signal. He ran his hands through his red-blond hair, looked at Amon, looked at Brace. Lamp was like a man doing laborious sums and wishing for an adding machine. He arrived at a total, seemed stunned, re-checked his figures.

"Out," he said to Brace. "Get off of this messdeck."

"What?"

"Get off of my messdeck. You're causing this." The hysteria that trembled in Lamp's voice seemed to free him. He reached for Brace, who was still attempting to capture Amon's banging legs. He caught Brace's collar, pulled him backwardly erect. Brace attempted to turn, was thrown off balance by the corkscrew motion of the ship. He fell backward, bounced against a bulkhead, came slowly to his feet and stood bewildered. Lamp threw his huge body across Amon's legs, took a knee in the belly, struggled.

"Out," Lamp gasped.

"Take off," Howard said to Brace. "We'll get it figured later."

Brace stood as if testing catatonia of his own. He moved vaguely. He flushed with guilt or embarrassment, began to leave, stopped. He turned back, a man proven guilty by accusation. "Let's get it figured now," he said. "Let's get it figured right now, cook." He began to move forward, one hand clutching, one hand clenched. The huge, heavy-moving body of Lamp rose and fell with Amon's kicking.

"Out," said Wysczknowski. "I don't know what's going on, but that's an order, chum, that ain't just good advice."

Brace stood shocked, defeated. He turned to leave, turned back; more rebellious than the Old Testament Gideon, equally confused. His mouth trembled with a movement of jaw, a shudder of lips.

"You want to know how dumb I am," he said. "I thought this ship was different, that's how dumb I am. This place is just like every other place." He bounded away, up the ladder, bouncing in bruising crashes against bulkheads like a man selected for the pleasure of a demon.

"A Punch and Judy show," Howard told Wilson. "Things got settled down, but Amon still won't cross the fiddley."

"They talking to each other?"

"They're not even seeing each other. Dane won't let Brace on the messdeck. The kid is eating in the crew's compartment. Amon is sleeping in the galley."

"That can't last."

"No," Howard said. "We'll see what a doctor has to say about Amon."

"It's that bumboat," Wilson said mournfully. "Ever since we pulled it in."

Howard, having forgotten *Hester C.* as completely as he had forgotten his unknown father, gazed at the empty end of the pier like a voyager to far lands getting reacquainted with his hometown. He looked toward the channel, shook his head.

"I was belowdeck with that flyer when we came in."

"It got loose during the storm," Wilson told him. "It's over there on them mudflats just waitin' and watchin' us. It's going to be sitting on those mudflats forever."

XII

〰〰〰〰〰〰〰〰〰〰〰〰〰〰〰〰〰〰〰〰〰〰〰〰〰〰〰〰〰〰

STEAMING THROUGH September, *Adrian* resembled a toy ship playing at rescue. It towed the *Ann*, the *Emerald*, the *Dolphin*— two trawlers and a giddy-looking yacht that was rigged (as Fallon remarked) like a Paris lady's toilet. The tows were dull, short and routine. They were so easy that Levere occasionally left the bridge for a one-eyed nap. Seas ran nearly mellow. Winds retreated north as if to bide their time. Old men knit gear, eyed the north with suspicion, looked at the gray and motionless sea, while young men were lulled. The lousy cutter *Able*, of New Bedford, went aground on a sandbar off Martha's Vineyard and cleaned some barnacles from its hull. It was freed by the tide and a tow from an 83 boat. Men shook their heads as the tale spread through the fleet. They praised the good luck that found them only on the North Atlantic, and not on the cutter *Able*.

"Cutter Un-Able," Glass said. "Sell it to the Mexican navy."

"I don't want to hear," Lamp told him. "I got enough to think about."

Hester C. lay on the mudflats like a small black and gray splash of fear, or a low grade curse. A third yellow raft that was deflated and broken and flogged and thrown by the tide, came ashore near Kennebunkport. Levere received two letters. One was written by an Air Force squadron commander. The other was written by a widow. Levere wrote answers to the letters from the privacy of the wardroom.

Cutter *Aaron,* of Boston, towed a tugboat—which (as the red-headed Rodgers pointed out) was like letting a barmaid take the pope on a guided tour—while Snow said: "Lad, if you crack wise about my last ship, I must adjust you in a way that will make you forever innocent to barmaids."

Adrian was relieved from standby for a week. Men went ashore. They saw and smelled garlicky sailors from a French destroyer. The sailors wore red-trimmed hats, and they straddled bar stools with cocky and easy arrogance. They made wonderful conquests among the bar girls. *Adrian's* crew was too unjoyful to fight.

The Cape Cod Canal bridge stuck halfway up or halfway down. Rumor said that it looked like something—that when you saw it—you wanted to kick a field goal. Aboard an Italian freighter, a deckhand hanged himself from a steering cable. From northward came radio gossip about the early formation of ice.

Amon disappeared shoreward, to walk (when Lamp visited him) white-robed and in a bemused state along the polished floors of the Marine hospital.

"He knew me," Lamp reported. "I think he's going to be just fine."

After a week, a memorandum arrived. Amon had epilepsy. After a second week, Amon's orders arrived. He disappeared toward the interminable hospital circuit of Boston. Lamp, in mourning, packed Amon's gear for transit to the hospital. Lamp would accept no help. He would allow no one to enter the privacy of his grief. Men passed silently by him as he stood in the crew's compartment and rolled Amon's clothing into tidy bundles. Lamp occasionally untied a roll, then rolled it over and over again until he was satisfied that it was perfect. His small head, which was always disproportionate to his huge frame, now seemed of normal size as he slumped deeper and deeper into his clothing. He whispered to himself, or to Amon—or perhaps he prayed. The silent, passing men looked at each other, shook their heads, then climbed to the main deck and gave low and surprised whistles.

"You'd think the guy was dead," Conally said to Howard.

"Lamp and Amon worked together for a long time."

"I miss the little guy," Conally said. "I'm not sayin' that I don't miss him."

Like an erased spirit, Amon was scuffed from the messdeck and into the ditty bag of tales that were not sea stories, as Jensen's death was a sea story.

Men remember ships, but few departed men are remembered aboard ships. Although a man may walk straight across the pier and take duty on a neighbor ship, he seems to have ceased existence when his feet step for the last time from the gangway. His name is crossed from sailing lists, duty rosters, and, at best, he leaves a small and noticeable vacuum into which a new man with fresh orders will step.

"I hope the new guy's a Chinaman," Glass confided to Howard. "It might make Lamp feel better."

"There isn't any new guy. We don't have any orders, yet."

Lamp rarely spoke. When he did, it was in a graveside voice that shushed and offered sorrowful scorn. In somber tones he repeatedly observed that good men died young and bad ones were promoted. His gossiping, speculating and moral-headed self seemed withered, indrawn, or shelved like a dusty parcel of beans forgotten among the dry stores. He spoke of growing old, and his face drifted like a cratered moon about the galley. His eyes seemed to sink backward in their sockets as if, inside him, sight and soul were searching to combine. He told no stories. He refused to speak to Brace. Brace, through confusion or tact, avoided the messdeck. Lamp watched Brace's comings and goings. When Brace did appear, Lamp splashed hot water in his sinks, may have burned his hands, was obviously searching for heat.

Lamp worked, strove, attempted to do the work of three men and could not do the work of two. Work increased as Lamp's timing failed and the bottoms of pots and pans were burned and needed scouring. He was like a penitent answering for the sins of the entire crew, and perhaps answering for a few of his own. His cooking lapsed into a menu so terrible that radioman James (who claimed to have once suffered greatly) further claimed that eating aboard *Adrian* was like eating at home when you were married. Men who had never been married clung to their illusions. They scoffed at James. Like husbands they bore with Lamp's grief. Like lovers viewing that first momentous stumble, they expressed the firmest loyalty, but their eyes reflected small yet awful doubt.

Dane, who had seen ten dozen cooks, and who knew when a ship had a good one, assigned men from his deck gang to take turns at helping Lamp. Lamp scorned them, spoke in small shrieks, seemed compelled by the hysteria that attends the romance touted by popular magazines. He shrewishly told vigorous and adroit seamen that they were inept. They were clumsy. They could not peel a potato properly, nor wash dishes, nor could they fill the coffee urn without spilling. After Lamp served franks and beans for the third night in a row, even the most loyal of his husbands agreed that something had to be done.

Lesser deities might need ten, but Dane had one commandment. It concerned competence at sea. Conally lived easily beside Dane. Bosun striker Joyce lived through days of celebration or through days of dark failure. Seaman Glass, the best man aboard in his rating, rarely suffered. Brace, whose performance was a little bit better than bad, was still a pluckable chicken.

Dane spoke to Lamp. He talked not with a roar, but in the rough tones of comradeship assumed between men who have shared wind and heavy water. Lamp faltered. Dane was flustered. He had not expected a scene or a public display. Lamp stood in his galley and blubbered that he would earn atonement. Embarrassed men sidled from the messdeck. They fled with the rapid regret of refugees kicked from their homeland through differences between politicians. Lamp swore that he would do better.

He did worse. From a creature of indignation and remorse, he turned into a creature of confusion. His commissary lists brought strange combinations of stores to the fantail. Howard shook his head over requisitions and wondered why *Adrian* needed two cases of stove blacking. For the first time in Howard's memory, Dane had a command problem worth taking to Levere. The problem was discussed in the wardroom over plates filled with something that vaguely resembled frank and bean stew.

"Thought he'd shape up on his own," Dane said. "He's a rated petty officer. He ain't a kid."

"I called Personnel," Levere said. "No steward is available right now."

Howard listened from his customary position in the ship's office. He nearly choked from a gulp unattended by beans.

"We might have tolerated it last summer," Levere said. "Now the men are not getting much liberty."

"Nor are we," said Snow. "One forgets tranquillity when all is well."

"It ain't tran . . . quillit—it's chow. These guys' morale will get shot."

"Personnel can send a seaman apprentice."

"We already got an apprentice."

"You have heard the tale about Jensen?"

"Amon was getting sick," Levere said. "The crew knows he was seeing things."

"Some are a bit spooked."

Howard, who would be double-dog-damn before he would admit that he had also seen Jensen, sat silent.

"I don't want to transfer Lamp," said Levere. "He deserves better. We won't get a replacement as good."

"I tried givin' him a shake. He shakes too easy."

"He needs permanent help. Assign your junior man until we can get a steward."

"Lamp won't have that kid on a bet. Lamp is down on that sailor."

"Lamp needs a new set of problems," Levere told Dane. "One way to cure a rift is to make men work together."

". . . one way to kill a punk." Dane was reluctant. "Sorry, cap."

"No, give me your opinion."

"I've been shovin' the kid's nose in it for six months. He's startin' to come around."

"He wishes to be an engineer," said Snow. "We could put it to him that success with Lamp is a route to the engine room. If Chief Dane agrees."

". . . if it's for the good of the ship . . . these kids come and go . . ."

"He may eventually change his mind about the engine room," Levere said. "These youngsters are flighty."

Brace went to the galley, to the hot and steaming crucible a-rattle with pans, loud crashes beside Lamp's huge silence and peremptory commands. Brace discovered red-tiled decks, bleached walkboards to be pulled and scrubbed daily, sinks floating a thin skim of grease, the smell of fresh garbage, of onions, and the pale sight of cod, halibut, and the red slabs cut from animals. Silence amplified the rattle of lobsters in a bucket, a gift to the menu from a towed lobsterman who felt that he needed to insure good credit; or was possibly grateful. In the wardroom and on the messdeck Brace dealt with the nose-wrinkling smell of brass polish, the bland smell of soap, starch, and the acrid disinfectant; the whole knit together in its many parts by Swedish steam and brooded over, it seemed, by the coffee urn which sat as idollike as a well-burnished commodore. Sliced potatoes were peeled in a vat of cold water . . .

"I hate it," Brace told Howard, "but I can hold out for awhile."

"We only get stewards when somebody enlists from Hawaii."

"The engine room," said Brace. "No more freezing, no more Dane."

"Dane is okay. What do you know about freezing?"

"He's not okay," Brace said. "He's a secret trombone player"; and Howard, a day or two later, thought of the summer and of Brace's tale. Howard dismissed the matter for a week as he thought of other things, and as *Adrian* steamed into a haunted October. Howard returned to Brace.

"Why the engine room?"

"Snow."

"He's the guy who smacked you."

Brace, having wrestled deeply with philosophic problems while painting the mast, did not realize that his solution was old and unmentionable news. He began a grave summation. "He was tryin' to tell me what was important."

"You should be a Philadelphia lawyer, kid."

" . . . not much is . . . important. I can hold out for a while."

"We get another steward, then maybe you're off the pick."

Chagrined, Lamp made the best of a bad case. He turned hotly from the insoluble problem of Amon, to the close and burning problem of personal insult. When Brace's name disappeared from the watch list, Lamp muttered to Howard about plots. When Dane told Lamp that Brace was to be his new helper, Lamp affected catatonia of his own. His eyes blinked, his lower lip quivered—and, when Dane went back abovedecks, and the constrained landscape of the messdeck seemed unlikely to launch tigers or chief bosuns, Lamp bustled to the ship's office and threatened in outspoken terms about a transfer. His face flushed, his hips moved in humorous and slightly lewd wiggles of agitation. His honest despair combined with his dishonest threats and he was like pink pie-filling oozing through a crust of sorrow.

"Cutter *Able* needs a cook," said Howard. "Cutter *Able* always needs a cook."

"Don't smart-mouth, sonny."

"And a crew. And a captain."

"I can go to any ship in this district."

"The lightship needs a cook. Easy duty. Ride on those mushroom anchors all year. A lot of vomit, a little soup. Gets so you can't tell the difference."

"You're worse than Glass. Glass is only evil, but you—you . . ."

Lamp's revenge was silence. It was like Quaker revenge, or it was oriental, and it carried, naturally, more power than any Protestant dialectic. It was the righteous silence of predestination flogged by ill omen. Or, perhaps, it was the silence of the defeated general, the politician made ludicrous, the embezzling banker caught rifling his mortgages and his plans to seduce widows in advance of foreclosure. Lamp huffed and he puffed, and seemed swollen with air in his attempt to suppress words; like he had gulped a huge wind that he judiciously withheld until the proper moment to blow down the house of cards that life had dealt. Instead of nagging Brace, he gave curt commands about business. Brusque orders made Brace trot, but the quality of Lamp's cooking improved. The lost Amon no longer seemed to chatter quite so close to Lamp's ear.

"He won't be able to hold out," Glass said.

"I doubt it," Howard agreed. "He wants the engine room pretty bad, but nobody could put up with that."

"I mean Lamp. I know that big ox. Once he starts to talking it's all over."

As if to prove Glass correct—and suddenly—one morning it

was all over. Howard returned from a mail run to the Base in company with yeoman Wilson. Howard heard a voice as he descended the ladder, and the voice was like a heavy-shanked memory of hours and days and weeks and months of gossip, idiocy and small wisdom. Words spilled, flooded, took roundhouse swings at silence. Lamp was telling Brace about riots and low acts in Hong Kong. Howard grinned, chuckled with relief, and headed for the office not yet knowing what *Adrian* lay athwart that ghastly October.

XIII

MIST THAT carried its own gray chill blanketed
October as it covered the lengthening nights, and shrouded and
cloaked the mornings. From across the harbor in Portland, a
faint glow occasionally reached toward the man on watch as he
stared into the cold blanket of night, and the glow which should
have seemed warm, was like phosphorescence. The mist played
at becoming fog, made atmospheric transubstantiations, rolled
in the center of the harbor even when the land was for a few
hours free. The fog looked like a band of dark gray gauze, and it
hovered low over the channel so that men on watch during the
day occasionally saw a masthead floating above the fog, dis-
connected, as if it had been freed by an axe of medieval justice.
The mist swelled from the mudflats at dusk and moved upward
about the broken *Hester C.* The hulk sat in a cauldron of mist.
The mist seemed trying to grasp and lift the thing to a steady
keel and to a spirit's float through the wet gray muff of air that
pocketed ships and warmed only by contrast, as men hastened
their chores on deck and ducked back through hurriedly un-

dogged hatches into the warmth of the ship. As cold daylight gave over to colder night, the mist turned into ice fog so that about the decks slicks appeared in patches. Ladders from decks to bridges were rimed with ice by their separated exposure. The ice lay in the cleats of ladders like an extra coat of paint. In other pockets of cold the mist accumulated, formed drops larger than tears but smaller than eyes. The drops froze into frosty white pebbles like seed pearls and men flicked them from the rails and chains with forefingers, as though they were shooting a game of marbles with the fog.

Cutter *Abner* received a proceed-and-assist to aid the venerable fishing vessel *Enoch,* and *Abner's* stern melted whitely into the gray, liquefying mist like an old pilgrim accustomed to his treacherous path. *Adrian* received a proceed-and-assist on *Tinker Bell* and found it drifting in the veil of mist with sails still set and stiff with ice, as the mist, unimpressed by the frivolity of names, clustered in a nimbus about *Tinker Bell's* running lights while an hysterical yachtsman, his hysterical crew, and his voluptuous and also hysterical companion yelled, hollered, bawled, and pledged fealty, ever after, to the sanctuary of Florida's waters.

Cutter *Abner* received a proceed-and-assist to carry a mechanic and repair parts to the coastal tanker *Asteroid. Abner* delivered, and then stood by during the hours of repair. *Abner* hovered on the gray sea in a light swell, forefoot meeting the rise of water with the deliberately stepping piety of an old desert father among dunes. *Adrian* received a proceed-and-assist on fishing vessel *Ephraim,* then, lengthening the tow while men stood at the rail with a stretcher, picked up a heart attack victim from Orrs Island as *Adrian* returned to harbor. The heart attack man was old, pale and afraid. His face was gaunt and exact and unconfused with his fear. Beneath the red lights of the wardroom, his face was as certain as an icon—although he gasped. Howard did not know what to do for him, and Snow did not know, either; but, when the heart attack man was taken away in an ambulance at the South Portland pier, he was still alive. Howard and Snow breathed more fully, resolved to find out if somewhere there was a book that discussed hearts; and the rest of *Adrian*'s crew breathed more fully as well.

"It's a good sign," Lamp confided to Howard and Racca. "The signs are all mixed, but that's a good one."

"You're mixed, cook," said Racca. "The only signs I believe in are beer signs."

"It's the weather," Lamp said to Howard. Lamp tossed his head in a sniffy way that dismissed the rude Racca. "All this fog. There should be more wind. By now it should be howlin'."

"We ought to be getting more wind," Howard admitted, "but what's the big deal about fog?"

"I ain't a kid," said Lamp. "I knew a guy did duty on the *Bear*."

"Sure you did, an' I knew Big Foot Tilton."

"Those old-timers knew fog. There's bad things happen in fog."

"There's bad things happen in bars."

"Puget Sound weather."

"I never been west of Peoria," Racca said with malicious contentment. "I don't even believe in the Mississippi River."

Cutter *Aaron* of Boston laid line aboard the fishing vessel *Lydia*. Cutter *Amos* of Portsmouth caught a double, towing the *Patty L.* and the *Joy*. The lousy cutter *Able*, of New Bedford, searched for two boys in a dory that had been carried away by the tide. *Able* sent breathless, flank speed reports for sixty hours until one of the boys was picked up by trawler *Victoria* twenty miles from *Able*'s search pattern.

"Kids. A kid."

"I hate that box."

"*You* hate that box? I'm from Massachusetts where we really *know* how to hate." Glass, that easy admirer of grand theft, stood in white-faced and speechless helplessness.

In the third week of October, the mist seemed to exert itself in a great piling-on that saturated the air, so that on deck men felt drops and splatters on faces and jackets as the mist spilled in pats of nearly frozen water. The decks were wicked with thin ice. The very sky demonstrated that only so much water could be held in solution with air, and the drops were not rain, but spilled and overflowing mist.

Adrian, groping dead slow among the islands, searched for the overdue lobsterman *Hattie*, reversed course and moved on whistle, bell, and local knowledge to check a radar contact a hundred yards astern. The contact was a gallon can that had once held dry milk. As *Adrian* put back around, yells and a thin whistle sounded from the fog where *Hattie* rode the pick at two hundred yards and made no image on the radar. The fog muffled the radar, and even the islands did not always give a hard contact. The radar was capricious, unworthy, and men stood in the bow and peered into fog and listened above the slow-breaking whisper of the bow wave. At night in fog, a man could not see beyond his eyelids. Conally swore that he was growing a third ear.

"Like the belly of a whale."

"Blacked out like a raided cathouse."

"It'd confuse a cat, boys. Even a ship's cat."

"Ship's cat is just an ordinary cat, cook. They ain't no cat comes with a label saying this'n is a ship's cat."

"You don't know cats," Lamp said. "If you don't know a blamed thing about cats, what do you know?"

"Cook's right," said Fallon. "I saw a ordinary cat jump off a fishing boat once. Went aboard for the smell, the boat got underway. Cat committed suicide."

Adrian groped through October. Men began to swear that even wind was better than the continuing, unnatural fog. Brace was as obscure as the weather. Like Amon before him, Brace spent long days in the midst of the crew's off-time banter. Like Amon, he walked through that center but found himself always on the periphery. He was segregated by his task, remote,

116

isolated from ship's routine by the dull round of his soap-slopping job. His work began at 0500 and was constant and dull and filled with Lamp's chatter and with messdeck gossip until 1900. He lived through a banal succession of days in which he heard about fog and mist, but saw it only when he took coffee to the bridge, or when he dumped garbage and washed the cans. He alternated cook's watch with Lamp, who was religious about supplying watchstander coffee and sandwiches at sea. Brace bore the tedium, and he always looked a bit soapy, a trifle too well washed. He was moody, subject to carping complaint and short-tempered whimsy. Lamp alternately rode him and appeased him.

"It's tough for a white man," Lamp told Howard. "But he could be doing lots worse."

Howard, who was vaguely democratic, wondered to Lamp if it was not tough for a dark man.

"It's a chicken job," Lamp said. "Most white guys have big ideas."

"Amon didn't?" Howard asked, then wished he had not.

"Amon had ideas. He just had different ideas." Lamp seemed momentarily withdrawn into private and raw pain. Then he shrugged to dissolve the past. In sporadic, interrupted conversation during the two days it took to find and tow *Hattie*, Lamp stated his theory of origins. The liberal Howard nodded his head, thought of immense matters, and did not listen at all. Howard was watching Conally, was testing himself, and was wondering if both of them were not mad.

The Indian Conally came from bow watch on the first day of the search for *Hattie*. He drew coffee, sat on the messdeck, and he looked like an upright burial. Conally seemed to be listening to the faraway whistle of *Adrian* that echoed from forward like a vibration instead of a sound. Dane tromped to the messdeck. *Adrian* rode on an even keel over flat, inshore water as it poked about the islands while the bridge gang peered into the radar and mistrusted the rapid, busy clicking of the fathometer.

Under conditions of smooth water, ship's work could be done. Dane tipped his chief's hat to the back of his head. He flipped mist from his upper lip with the back of his hand, rubbed at his nose with passing enjoyment. Dane stood as squat and certain as a hymn book. Conally sat like a parable.

"You sprain another ankle?"

"No."

"Messin' with that Peak's Island girl?"

"I ain't caught nothin'." Conally's black hair was double-colored with black. Where his watch cap had covered, the dry and stringy hair seemed nearly dull. Where the watch cap did not cover, his hair was glossy and slick with mist.

"If you ain't got a busted leg, and you ain't got a dose, then why are you loafin'?" Dane was a man for whom all things were certain. He no more expected moodiness from Conally than he expected a hippopotamus to come strolling across the messdeck.

Conally sipped at the coffee instead of slurping. He did not stand, and he did not move, and he did not give the impression that he was in any hurry to do either. "Caught a chill." The lie was so clumsy that even Conally did not buy it. *Adrian*'s whistle vibrated from forward. Conally flushed, high color on his cheeks that denied the rest of his dark face which seemed washed and sick and untribal.

"Old ladies get chills. Poodles get chills."

"I ain't a poodle, and not an old lady. Give it a rest."

Dane, stunned by rebellion from his star bosun, gasped like he had been hit with a dead fish. Then his eyes became squinty and he recognized that Conally really did look unnerved. Dane seemed ready to sit beside Conally, question him. It was not Dane's nature. Dane grumped. He looked like a troll. "When you get done enjoyin' your chill, set the gang to cleanup forward." Dane turned, began to move away, turned back. "I'll be on the bridge." It was large sympathy cloaked in small words, and it was the best that Dane could do.

Four hours later Howard returned from bow watch to the messdeck, drew coffee, sipped instead of slurping, and watched his hand tremble so that the heavy mug made a delicate tattoo, a chatter, against his teeth. In the galley Lamp told a long story about the hard-luck icebreaker *Eastwind*. Brace sat at a messdeck table trying out baseball grips on an onion. He gave dull responses of reluctant admiration on the subject of icebreakers. Wysczknowski laid out a hand of solitaire. From forward the whistle vibrated.

A man who sits and counts pennies in a YMCA room on Saturday night is not as lonely as a man standing watch in mist. Voices of horns, sirens and surf are remote because of the mist. Sounds are velvetly enclosed, obstructed. The ears feel plugged with velvet. Experienced men open their mouths to gather sound, and suffer mist on their tongues, feel absurd with jaws a-dangle, feel vulnerable in their throats as if soft and small and rancid creatures are flying in the mist searching to make a cold nest. The ship's whistle, making fog signals, intermittently squalls like a prehistoric animal. To say that a man is shrouded is to suggest the easy comfort of the grave, where, after all, there are no questions. In mist the questions assail, whisper, lightly touch the perceptions like fingernails of a frigid lover greeting warm intent with small protest. The shushing, hissing bow wave seems timid with the threat of impotence. Those terms of the sea which cleave and interpenetrate are plain silly in mist, for when the fathometer gives a readout of six feet the readout is only more or less. Winters on the coast of Maine are startling. The previous year's winter will have caused the chart to become an approximation, even with *Notices to Mariners*; a partly informed but hopeful opinion. Hulks have shifted position. Rocks have tumbled. Underwater chasms have accumulated the debris of error, and they twist currents with the force of a revised doctrine. In short: mist, and watchstanding in mist, along that rocky coast, are not a shroud of finality. It is the broad and fey fabric of awful possibility.

Howard sat on the messdeck after his watch and shuddered and giggled at the tremble in his hands. He stuck an index finger into the coffee to see if the finger was still alive. Then, like a smart robot who has just discovered originating thought, or like an idiot uncovering a reason for slobbering, Howard took off his foul-weather jacket and laid it on the bench beside him. He examined the right shoulder of the jacket with close and minute attention, searched for the impress of awful fingers, the marks of a dead world where air was always mist, and where mist was the supporting surface for weightless feet.

In the bow, anticipating his relief, and with his tongue licking mist from teeth and lips, Howard's first thought was that Glass silently approached to take the watch. In that unspoken code of men pressed together in close quarters, Glass had never before touched Howard. Glass had firm hands, no doubt, but Howard—who would have been shocked had he ever thought about the matter—would not have concluded that Glass had stern hands. The hand that silently gripped Howard's shoulder was as unremitting as bone.

Howard turned to complain to Glass, but, of course, there were some codes that even Glass did not break. Howard turned to find that Glass had not yet arrived, nor had anyone else. The mist swirled, the whistle arrowed into the mist like a screech of despair.

Howard looked all around him, saw Glass approaching, and found that a help. Howard managed not to run and shriek. He mumbled to Glass, went below to the messdeck after cowardly telling Glass that all was routine.

Brace slopped at tables with a wet rag. From forward the whistle vibrated. Howard watched Brace, that outlander to the messdeck, and Howard shuddered from fear or premonition, or because it seemed to him that he had never really looked at Brace before. Howard's teeth ticked and clicked against the coffee mug. Being aboard *Adrian* was not like being in Illinois. It was not like being in Ohio, either.

120

XIV

~~~~~~

THE APPARITION seemed born of werelight, and, as if no cock would ever crow the dawn, it took its time a-building. It came from *Hester C.*, which lay canted on the mudflats. Later on, no man could tell at which pointing, mincing moment the manifestation shook like a rumple-furred dog and detached itself from the mist. Some men did not see the apparition at all.

In later years, cooking at the Base, Lamp would claim that he was the first man to see Jensen, and he would believe it. Lamp's interpretation rose from that spacious imagination that swelled like a circus balloon filling his huge frame, giving reason for that frame's existence. Lamp actually saw nothing for several days, or rather, he saw no apparition. Nor did Brace.

"I thought it was a reflection at first," Glass told Howard after enough time had passed to still Glass's trembling.

Adrian had once more swung against the pier. Cutter *Abner* had disappeared into the mist, having towed *Theresa* into Gloucester, then caught a search to the south in company with the lousy cutter *Able*. Men joked, made sympathetic noises in behalf of *Abner's* crew. Gunner Majors claimed that *Able* was searching for the overdue yacht *Seascamp*, and *Abner* was sent along to keep *Able* from getting lost. It was a dull joke, made even more dull because of a general suspicion that it described the facts.

"I'm trying to convince myself that it was a reflection." Howard acted like a man prepared to bargain his half interest in the hereafter in return for the assurance of a reasonable world.

"Reflection of what? That's what I want to know," Glass said. "Reflection of what?"

Glass had been standing the in-port midwatch on the bridge in a muffled night of foghorns and the crackle of the radio. Lamp was resting his well-exercised tongue under the fog of sleep. Mist swirled about *Adrian* and was cut by a light breeze. The mist lifted in small whirls, gave way to narrow views and tunnels of clear darkness. It was like paint being stirred, folding in smooth swells that colored and became more solid with the mixing. Glass, having lived for so long with the mist, was bored, unimpressed, but he logged the fact of the breeze with some interest. He would have said, and did, that the breeze put different odds on the tote board.

The breeze was not a dancer. It held no cyclonic persuasions. It was interrupted. Sporadic. If it swirled, it did so because of broken flow that bent around buildings and vessels. Glass, in cynical sureness of the value of prophecy, would not ordinarily bet ten cents on a race that was fixed. Still, Glass was a child of New England. He shivered on the warm bridge, while the radio crackled, chattered, buzzed. Glass later confided to Lamp that he felt like "saying a little more about that breeze." Since he did not know what to say, he simply logged it.

The breeze folded the mist, opened dark and narrow alleyways down which a man might peer, then closed the far entry, as if it were blocked by the appearance of a blacked-out and prowling police car.

A pale light appeared on the mudflats where it was not possible that a light could be. It was like foxfire, luminous, indifferently unblinking as it flavored only itself while not revealing its surroundings. The light came and went and came and went, as mist ran in small torrents across the mudflats. Glass reached for a pencil, looked at the log, looked at his hump nose beneath untidy and lengthening hair reflected on the blacked-out screen of the radar, which behind its open mask took a faint sheen of red light from the night bulbs. Glass laid the pencil down, picked up binoculars. The light expanded, contracted, seemed in an effort of concentration. Glass watched, put the binoculars aside, picked up the telescope, although *Hester C.* lay within three hundred yards. The light was coming from the hulk. As Glass watched, it began to change, focus, become more incandescent.

"Like a work light," Glass told Lamp. "Like when you see one-a these lobstermen putting over traps after dark. It was even swinging, like he was riding a swell."

The mist whirled, swept, cloaked; and, through the wavering telescope, revealed a figure bent over the engine box. The figure was shadowed by the sideways cant of *Hester C.* The unwalkable deck seemed not to affect the figure at all. Glass would swear that if the thing had feet, it was using them to walk on mist. The figure was vague. It busied itself with its own concerns. It seemed to be drawn into the framework of the hulk, or into the engine box. Then it would rise as if attempting to step free of the wreck. Glass saw arms that waved in despair or struggle. The mist closed down, opened, closed.

Glass checked the watch list. The sarcastic Racca was in the engine room. Glass pressed a buzzer beside a voice pipe.

"Get up here. On the double."

"Can't leave the station. We're on generator."

"Move it. Move it."

Racca entered the bridge, took the telescope, looked.

"I'm going below."

"You see it?"

"And I'm staying below. For always. You've done some crazy things, Glass, but this cuts it." Racca's face was the color of whey, or at least it was that color when Dane later called him back to the bridge.

Glass, having once before woken Conally on the subject of *Hester C.*, went to the crew's compartment to wake him again. Glass thumped down the ladder with loud indifference to all sleepers.

"This better be good." Conally came from sleep, and he moved like a man half afraid, half joyous over some grim confirmation. As he passed Howard's sack, Conally shook Howard.

"You've had something on your mind, chum."

"It's not my watch."

"Get movin'. Glass caught hisself a ghost."

Howard found himself staring, wide-eyed, awake. "Something funny's been going on."

"Somethin's going on, but it ain't funny."

"I'm surrounded by experts," Glass chattered.

Fallon snorted, snorked, came awake. "What? What?" He rolled out, began pulling on his pants, then followed.

The mist was updrafting, back-flowing, like cold layers of slag magically unfrozen. There were cliffs and crevices in the mist; hollows, arroyos, switchbacks. It seemed geologic, and it seemed like the indifferent sweep of time or timelessness that chews planets into forms of dark mountains and dark seas.

"You see it, you see it there?"

"Call Dane. On the double."

"Log it."

"Don't log it. You crazy? Log it and you got it."

"What do you reckon?"

"It's fightin' to get loose."

"What is it? What?"

"That lobster guy, I think."

"I don't think so," Fallon said. "I don't know what I think." He lowered a set of binoculars, and his keglike shape seemed suddenly frail, thin. "We're doin' okay," he said in a voice wrung from fear. "We're makin' it." He seemed to be pleading with a friend.

A burst of static came from the radio, like chattering teeth, and, muted by mist, the commission pennant tapped from high above the heads of confused and frightened men. On the mudflats the arms waved, grasped, groped in undisguised battle as the creature struggled. The mist opened, closed.

"It's swelling. Gettin' bigger."

The mist closed over the bright light, opened again, and when Dane arrived on the bridge like a startled frog a-jump from a known and comfortable river bank, the bright light was dimming to luminosity. Dane looked at Conally, at Fallon. Dane's expression changed. His face no longer held the opinion that he had been woken by some punk seaman having dreams.

"There," Conally said. "Right over there."

Dane wrinkled his flat nose. "It's lights from the million dollar bridge. The mist cleared aft, and the bridge is glowin' at us." He looked at Conally, at Fallon. "Tell me."

Conally told him. " . . . and it's walking in that mist right now."

"Then you got no trouble, right?"

"A'course we got trouble," said Fallon. "What's it mean?"

"Smell the breeze."

"Wind?"

"No fog by morning," Dane said. "It's just this minute come onto winter."

Howard's voice was as querulous as a child begging to be spanked. "That has nothing to do with it. What does that have to do with it?"

"If it's walkin' in the mist, and if there ain't no mist, then you got no trouble, right?"

"I have trouble," Glass admitted with perfect diction. "I am not going to stand this watch alone."

"You'll stand it on top of the mast if I say so." Without his chief's hat, Dane seemed not as bulky or tough. Thin strings of hair, and most of them white, lay across his skull like a tangle of webbing spun by a committee of spiders. His rolled shirt sleeves revealed thick wrists, heavy hands, and his fingers were tapping some invisible surface. He looked like a man digging through his ditty bag of tales. He discovered the memory he sought. He looked at Glass, at Conally. "Stuff like this happens. I never seen it mean nothin' yet."

"It means something," Fallon said. "You didn't see it, chief."

Dane, whose one law was competence, looked at Fallon, who had spent a winter running the engine room after the drowning of Jensen. Dane seemed to be mentally turning over the tale dredged from memory. "It means one thing. Crews get spooked if their main guys get spooked."

Fallon hesitated, thought himself toward a brief jolt of understanding.

Dane turned back to Glass. "Relieve the engine room." He turned back to Fallon. "When your punk Racca gets here, square him away." To Howard and Conally he said, "Set double watches. Kiddies get lonely." Dane gave a vague snort, for a moment seemed indecisive. Then he gave a full blown and heavy snort, the contempt falling back into his voice as surely as any actor pulling on his mask of role before stepping toward a familiar stage. "I was on an icebreaker once. You punks don't know nothin' a-tall about winter." He went below, stomping, as though feet could hammer nails of certainty through the brains of uncertain and tremulous men who stood on the bridge, watched each other, looked at the dark mudflats, and concealed from each other their private tremors.

XV

THAT MAN with a propensity for miracles, that Lamp, whose job it was to know what fits in those spaces between groin and heart, took the news hard when he woke. Instead of chatter, of boisterous soothsaying because his grim views were proving out, Lamp fought back. He told Brace to "get crackin"; and Brace hustled, complained, was always three steps behind Lamp, who behaved like a man in combat. Lamp challenged the miraculous with bacon, sausage, beef, ham, eggs, biscuits, gravy, fresh fruit, cold juices, and a vat of hot chocolate made from stores cached back in anticipation of holidays. Brace dashed about like a complaining sea sprite, one burdened with tasks that whirled his planet backward. There were not enough pots, pans, peeled potatoes. Men who were accustomed to eating rapidly sat on the messdeck and felt the small plunge of *Adrian* in the freshening breeze. They helped Brace along with their chortles, smart remarks; and they chewed and chomped and burped and chewed some more, as though it were Christmas.

Lamp had "a feelin," as he confided to Howard, and Lamp was doing something about his feeling. Even Howard had to admit that the mist ridden night seemed a little silly when remembered across a full plate—and with gravy, too. "Like that time in Hong Kong," Lamp confided to Howard. "The cook coulda pulled that one out."

"What happened in Hong Kong?"

"Later. I'll tell you later," and Lamp bustled, charged his enemy, attacking the invisible through a smokescreen of whipped cream for men to smear over pie. "It's almost a relief," he told Howard. "We know we got a fight. It ain't skiddy, now."

Brace scrubbed pots, to see them immediately refilled. He was jolted into astonishment when the penurious Lamp railed at him to use an extra ration of coffee. Lamp squandered his commissary allowance like a man ashore with heavy pockets and a backlog of fantasies. Brace seemed suddenly grown thin of ambition, indifferent to lost hopes, and with mild distaste for all worlds including engine rooms.

"We'd ought to have a ghost more often," Racca said. "We'd ought to have one every day."

"You were scared three points off your compass," Glass told him. "You're a tough dago, Racca."

"Especially around yids. Especially."

And, as if it were Christmas, Levere, Snow and Dane stepped from wardroom to messdeck, found space, and celebrated in a vague manner. Levere was serene but not withdrawn. Snow rode Racca and Fallon with small jokes. Only Dane was reserved. He watched Lamp, and his satisfied opinion showed only in a slight, forward shifting of his toadlike frame. Dane may or may not have known Lamp's motives, but Dane liked what he saw.

As the freshening breeze kicked and moved *Adrian* against the pier, men relaxed with the tranquil readiness of sleeping cats. For some men, portent lived on an instinctive level. For other men, portent lived in the memory of harsh experience.

"It'll be a yacht," Conally said, "and it'll be today, and it'll be nightfall or a little after."

"Don't talk. Why ask trouble?"

"Summer sailors."

"They always get caught. Count on it."

"Yacht from the Virgin Islands," Racca said. "Nothing but virgins aboard. Been at sea for three months gettin' lonesome . . ."

"What would you know about virgins?"

Storm warnings never occur on a clear day, and as the light dulls into darkness in the northeast, and as the temperature crashes down like an anchor, vessels within reach of the coast make high-speed dashes to shelter. The channel lays a sharply pitching road for the pilot boat that heads seaward with pilots to meet more than one ship. A noble government—that is made of the firmest stuff—protects its cannon. From the sea-reaches come minelayers and destroyers, bulking rakish and gray against the dark sky as they head for the anchorage. The wind rushes, as if the continent has become a sudden vacuum, and the wind begins to howl above piling water. It does not moan, has no choreography, is only wind raised to a pitch of storm that denies any pretense toward music. In a while the howl will change to a scream, and the scream will be indifferent, although it seems, sometimes, to speak the name of a particular ship or a particular man.

Adrian bumped and banged against its fenders. The crew belched, yawned, hesitated with reluctance toward movement that, when it began, would be totally absorbing and would allow no quarter even for a single belch. Conally stretched, stood; his face an Indian mask of veiled intent, or of preoccupation with securing the decks. Howard, his belly tightly pressed against his belt, shrugged into his foul-weather jacket which carried a multitude of stains but no fingerprints. He left the messdeck to buck into the increasing wind as he went to the Base for the mail. He returned, opened the few envelopes, and discovered that Brace was off the hook. Somewhere en route, steward apprentice Iris was ordered to *Adrian*.

"What kind of a name is Iris?" Lamp asked when Howard called him to the office.

"An easy-to-spell name . . . how should I know?"

"I'll miss that Brace. That's no bad kid."

"Levere says not to tell him yet. Let it ride. Otherwise you won't get anything out of him."

"I can always get something out of him," Lamp said. "If I want to, I can get work out of any guy."

Howard, having loosened his belt and found that his waistband was still tight, was in no mood to disagree.

"You got a minute?"

"Sure."

"What happened in Hong Kong?"

"The crew on a Navy can went asiatic." Lamp leaned against the frame of the hatch as *Adrian*'s deck slid sideways in small, unexciting movements that were brought up short by the mooring. For the moment, at least, and having temporarily worked himself out of a job, Lamp had every reason to tell a sea story complete with embroidery, with moral twinges and judgment. His face settled in that direction. Then he seemed revolted by the idea. The directness of his morning's labor was a contradiction to ample rambling. His face, which was naturally red beneath the red-blond hair, was also red from the steam of boiling pots and the heat of his small galley which no fan could clear. For a moment Lamp looked nearly wise.

"You remember how things got skiddy awhile back?"

"Yes. Well, no."

"Things were disappearing."

"Yes."

"The same thing happened on that can. They'd been on station a long time. The officers were as nuts as the crew." Lamp looked like he was going to apologize for something, then did apologize. "I'm not saying that our boys are that way."

130

"What are you saying?"

"They beat a Chinaman," Lamp said with genuine unease. "Only they beat him too hard. They had to toss him overboard to hide it."

"Well . . . well, what?" Howard, who would have sworn that he could deal with reality, jumped mentally sideways. "They needed somebody to lynch. Ask McClean. Happens all the time in Mississippi."

"He was just a guy trying to make a livin'. He was just a guy who came aboard every day with fresh stores." Lamp seemed nearly as stalled by his story as was Howard. "It's the way it built up," he said. "The cook could of saved it, but he was asiatic as the rest."

"I don't know what you're trying to say."

Lamp looked suddenly shy, timid. "You think I fool around with stuff, and maybe I do. But we're gettin' some kind of sign."

"Bad luck?"

"I just know how bad it can get. I can fight that part, anyway." Lamp began backing from the office, one hand resting on the frame of the hatch. "They claimed that Chinaman was bad luck. The whole deal got hushed up. An officer was in on it." He backed away further, then turned and nearly fled, a man who had gossiped about a memory for so long that he had forgotten that the memory was stark.

As a storm increases, ships fleeing past the Portland Head, chased by hugely running swells and by wind that raises shrieks in their rigging, have sometimes stumbled on the tide. The bottom builds out there. When conditions are exactly wrong, huge rocks are flung in grenades of water to explode high above the cliff where lore has it that they have occasionally knocked out the light. There is not much bottom. Small ships are twisted, flung, the helm a feeble protest when a fast-ebbing tide meets a full, incoming storm. It is like a giant roller coaster in an uncertain and macabre amusement park where tracks lead over the hump, come arcing down, and disappear into rock. Large ships have been gutted. Small ships, catching conditions that are exactly wrong, roll over. They offer a fast flurry of spray, a small contribution to that vast wealth of water that lies on the collection plate of the wind.

Yacht *Aphrodite*, schooner-rigged and not as old as mythology, but certainly as old as *Adrian*, and with a skipper who was no fool, confirmed Conally's prediction an hour ahead of schedule. *Aphrodite*'s hull was disproving the idea that sound maintenance on an ancient bucket will avoid catastrophe. A design that had once held notions of watertight integrity had been violated through redesign. *Aphrodite* was taking water forward through a sprung plate. It had one watertight bulkhead just forward of midships. It had good pumps, a captain who was a friend of Levere's . . . and, it carried a terrified owner who, downeast in Boston, was regarded as a valuable constituent. The man was "getting the cure" from the sea, which teaches that you cannot buy votes against a storm.

"Steel hull. A hundred thirty feet." Radioman James spoke to a small group on the messdeck. James was below for a quick sip of coffee before *Adrian*, crashing ahead slow on steadily warming engines, reached the approach to the head.

"Can we tow? Think of the draft on that thing."

"Don't know, chum. Maybe tow from the stern."

"Where's *Abner*?" Brace asked.

"Still playing pattycake down south. Still riding herd on *Able*."

Brace's eyes were bright with excitement. They held no fear. He had seen some weather, doubtless thought it was awful weather, doubtless believed he had seen the worst. He was filled with ignorant enthusiasm, excused, perhaps, because any kind of action no doubt seemed better than the dull promise of stewardship.

"Take a turn, sonny," Lamp told him. "When you get done whoopin', secure the wardroom."

132

Ships, following the romance of the sea with their grace and their resemblance to a womb, are said to embody a female principle; and the sea, itself, is called mistress, harlot, lover, mother.

Maine winters carry a different message. The ship is not soft, warm, loving or safe. The sea is what it is—the sea. *Adrian* was neither male nor female, but under the circumstances was something more important. *Adrian* was a ship. Designed by an architect long dead, twice redesigned by a tight-fisted Treasury . . . a Treasury that perhaps understood that experience teaches what a ship will take, but would never understand that only final experience teaches what it will not take.

McClean crept backward down the steps leading to the messdeck. He was spraddled flat as a starfish. The steps surged forward as McClean's arms stretched between rails, and for long moments he lay flat on his face as *Adrian* dove, took green water over the bridge, raised its stern, lay head down and shuddering beneath the heavy thunder of the sea. Lights flickered, flicked, from a generator where Wysczknowski stood by, lashed to the generator's cage. The ship slowly shrugged away water and sluggishly rose. McClean was pressed upright, nearly thrown backward, and an oily spot on his shirt made him look curiously like a man freshly shot. The lights steadied. From forward the thunder rumbled, decreased as the ship topped a swell, then rushed downward to another crack of thunder. McClean held on, again went forward on his face, wedging knees against the ladder, his forehead pressed down as if he was kowtowing to the sea, while his rear end struggled to get on the same level with his face. He starfished to the messdeck, turned and held on, waited in the boom and crash for the top of a swell. He dashed forward and hugged the coffee urn like a man in love.

Brace, white-faced, sat on a bench behind a table. He clutched the table. He was colorless except for his growing shock of hair. His face was bleached, then dim, then steadily bleached as from forward Wysczknowski temporarily settled matters with the generator.

McClean, his mulatto face not a whit darker than Brace's, looked frozen in an eternal scream like a masterwork of medieval fresco. Words that were faint, covered with thunder, "engine room . . . where's . . . yeoman—"

Brace clutched the table, stared at familiar, scrubbed bulkheads which always before had stood like planes of boredom. Now the bulkheads rose above his eyes like downrushing plates of steel. He seemed mesmerized, a man sillily gazing at his opposable thumbs in a universe that required tentacles.

McClean was sobbing, or else gasping for breath. He was certainly burning his arms on the coffee urn. A faraway crash of thunder was followed by a nearly present crack that was no louder, but more instantly threatening than the thumping, thundering, drumming sea. The crack came from directly above deck, the fantail.

Brace blinked, fought to stay erect against a downward surging crunch, stood blinking and grasping and no doubt wondering if it was time to drown.

"Gear locker," McClean yelled as *Adrian* reached the top of a swell. For three seconds his voice could be heard. "Engine room. Get there. Yeoman."

Howard appeared from his small sanctuary like a jumping jack not thrown by its spring, but thrown box and all by the hand of a petulant child. He grabbed the frame of the hatchway, leaned forward to stand spraddle-legged. He locked his hands onto that frame, as enamored of that frame as McClean was of the coffee urn. The men waited for the top of another swell.

"Busted arm . . . still on the plates—"

McClean turned, dived for a rail, began his slow, starfish ascent. *Adrian* hesitated, the dark, piling sea offering a crossswell to trick the helm. The ship was caught, twisted, skidded in a long slide; then fell like a tin safe dropped from the roof of a high building. It tipped to port, lay like a sick and dying fish; twisted feebly beneath the crash, the slow ascent. The world reversed. The ship skidded down, crashing, rolling, and the coffee urn like a gleaming inclinometer went horizontal. From beneath its clamped lid, coffee spurted like a small, round, laughing mouth. Brace stood spread against the table top, standing in desperation as Howard clung like a monkey on a stick to that rising and hovering frame. He lay on his back in the air and waited for the final, awful dictate. The shaft whipped, roared, the rudder caught, and the ship turned once more into the sea. The thunder began again, and Howard, who could not spare the luxury of relaxing any muscle, gulped air and wept and belched and choked up bile. He motioned to Brace. Brace, having frozen so hard to the table during his dance with the ship that he now lay on top of the table, dismounted and followed Howard, spraddling and starfishing up the ladder.

Racca, his smart mouth moaning, his shirt torn away, was held against the lightly oiled plates by men who kept him from flopping. Snow had Racca's broken arm extended. Howard crawled forward with the aid kit, off balance, bumping against a protecting rail beside the engine. Brace, off balance and crawling, bumped Howard from behind as Brace attempted to pass splints that were not yet needed. Racca's eyes were bright with fear and pain, and with the sharp hurt of helplessness as *Adrian* slid, thumped, and the voices of the engines were blanked even as he lay beside them; blanked by thunder from forward and the drum of the sea against the hull. Howard eased forward with a styrette of morphine, got the needle into the skin and crushed the small glass tube. Racca was looking at him or beyond him, talking, talking. Howard bent forward. Racca was saying, "Jonah, Jonah, Jonah," and Howard, who was not without guilts of his own, wondered if Racca was talking about him.

XVI

~~~~~~

THAT WORD, Jonah, that name—sparked in the minds and affrighted hearts of men, but the spark was dull and obscure during those first desperate night hours required for the wind to drop. The sea piled, ran as high as most men could ever remember having seen it run. As the wind dropped, the sea built. *Adrian* made heavy, tortured way. It buried its bows. Green water still reached the bridge, but water no longer swamped the flying bridge. On the flying bridge, the new shoring had disappeared from beneath light, stout cable. Speculation said that the entire bridge had been twisted, for the quick-release gear on the cable was still fastened. The flag locker was dented. The main deck was missing all but a single locker, but the winch was intact. The boat still hung in the davits like a small, white miracle. The 20-mm guns were wet beneath their waxed canvas covers. When Conally broke into the line locker, belowdecks and aft, he found an inch of water shipped through the seal of the watertight hatch. Conally swore to Howard that the inch of water was more scary than any ghost. That inch of water, although Conally did not say as much, was an insult to intelligence, like finding that the laws of gravity and flotation were repealed. Gunner Majors, who looked like a halfback ought to look, behaved like a halfback as he bounced about the boat deck. Majors was in definite hazard as he attempted to dry and oil those useless and silly guns. In the bow, the three-inch fifty had been stripped of its waterproof shroud. The muzzle plug was knocked out. Water filled the barrel. Water crashed and swept the gun as the water tumbled high to the bridge, and there was nothing Majors could do about that.

That word Jonah, that name—sparked from dull glow to brilliant, flashing fear as soon as the midwatch began.

Levere was a hawk-faced silhouette, more rigidly set in the high captain's chair than any welded fixture. Dane and Chappel alternated watches, and it was Chappel who took the mid. Belowdecks, Racca was strapped into his bunk, buzzy and drugged with codeine after the morph wore off. There was nothing to be done with Racca. One by one men dropped by his bunk, clung to the rail of the bunk, and joked to Racca, who was nearly unconscious and fairly beyond caring about anything but his one preoccupation. He hummed, sang the word, Jonah, in a dopey and drugged voice, and even Glass could not insult him enough to bring him to another subject. Howard substituted Brace's name for Racca's on the engine room watch list, and—there being nothing else that he could do, either—waited.

Where it came from, no man knew, but the spectre arrived as an independent mist walking across the water, or slightly above the water, like a wanderer across a barren planet, its meandering accidentally crossed by one of those ships doomed by myth to cruise an unending and haunted search. The spectre might have passed unnoticed in the night, or might have been mistaken for a dash of phosphoresence that lighted the dark, breaking sea.

Quartermaster Chappel checked his lights to see if he still had any. The searchlight on the port wing failed. Chappel sent word for electrician Wysczknowski to lay to the bridge. Bosun striker Joyce had the helm, and yeoman Howard was alternating radio and radar watch with James. Chappel entered the bridge from the port wing, where he had returned to fiddle the light. His horsey-looking head, his bent stance as he glanced at the plot, made him look like a mild-mannered piece of ivory trapped in a chaotic game of chess. The sea mounted from the bow, rode like a tide against the house, rose crashing in white and black shatters. Chappel's foul-weather gear was slick. When water dripped from his watch cap onto the chart, he seemed stricken with small pain. He dabbed at the blot with his handkerchief, probably the only handkerchief aboard.

"It may be a circuit," he said. "Permission to leave watch and check the starboard light."

Levere grunted. "I have the deck. Go ahead."

Chappel bent over the log and wrote meticulously in his accurate manner that was said to drive Dane crazy. Joyce spun the wheel, looked like a man searching for the meaning of life as he stared into the gyro repeater.

"Need a hand?" Howard asked Chappel.

"I believe you have the radio and radar watch. I believe there is traffic on the radio right now."

Howard turned the receiver higher. Through the static a voice was yammering, high-pitched and unreadable. The voice was faint, but while the words said nothing, the crackling, blanking static did not conceal the hysteria in the voice. "Stay on that," Chappel said, "as a matter of interest. Yes?" He undogged the hatch to the starboard wing, stepped through, and the wind swallowed his grumbles.

From such great distance there was nothing about that radio traffic that could affect *Adrian*, a ship already on a job. Howard listened in protest but with a bad conscience. Levere sat like a statue and faced the high speed wipers, a statue which heard every hearable sound.

" . . . Fox niner-seven," said the radio, and returned to its hysteric gabble. Howard leaned forward. From the helm came a small, uneasy movement from Joyce.

"Cutter *Able*," Levere said. "Let's have that box turned all the way up." Beneath the small glow of the starboard running light, Chappel's horse face was greenly blanched and bent low over the canvas cover of the searchlight. He released securing lines. Howard turned the receiver full, and the bridge was filled with the flak of static that gabbled, bubbled, spit and cracked. From the starboard wing the searchlight came on, and it threw a beam across the heaving, rolling, breaking sea. The beam began to shift as Chappel traversed the range of the light, checking meticulously.

"Gabble pop flak gabble fire," said the radio. "Lost puff," said the radio, "lost pow . . . ".

"Cap—"

"I heard it. Get Chappel in here."

The searchlight remained fixed and the spectre moved into the beam, walking, walking. *Adrian* pitched. Chappel met the movement and traversed. The spectre walked, walked. It moved across the tops of swells with the steady pace of a man on an errand.

"Belay that order," said Levere.

Joyce gave a small nicker of fear. He looked up, remembered the compass, spun the wheel.

"Cap."

"I see it."

Adrian pitched forward and the searchlight traversed. The spectre walked, and in the strong light the wrinkles of its clothing were unaffected by water. It was dry. The dungaree pants crimped at the back of the knee, and the dungaree shirt followed the swinging movement of arms. It was not possible in that light to see either more or less than what was there, and what was there was a set of sailor's dungarees walking without benefit of head, hands or feet. Howard gasped, had a happy and innocuous and stupid thought. He shifted the scale of the radar down to one mile range and hid his face in the mask. When he raised his head from the mask, the spectre was gone.

"No contact."

"I didn't expect one." Levere stood away from the captain's chair. He spoke as quietly as ever, but he—who had roamed every latitude of those northern waters and who would tell tales—was awed.

"Nan mike fox two-one from nan mike fox, priority." District radio, with its larger transmitter, came in clear.

"Callin' *Abner*."

"Fitz two-one," said the radio.

Howard reached for a message blank. On the wing, green shadowed, Chappel covered the searchlight. His lips moved in green and serious, dark-shadowed conversation with himself—or with the starboard running light, or with the sea. He worked rapidly, or as rapidly as a meticulous and ritualistic character could work.

"Information all floating units," said District, "information Officer in Charge New Bedford."

From the rear of the bridge, where he stood after having silently arrived, and shocking as a present spectre, electrician Wysczknowski gave a small moan, a terrible sigh. He watched heads jerk before him as if hit with a cattle prod. "Calling *Abner*," he said apologetically.

"If you ever do that again . . . . " Levere heard his own voice. "The port searchlight is out," he said, so quietly that his words were nearly swallowed in the crashing sound of water. "We'll need that light, directly."

The dogs on the hatch turned slowly as Chappel methodically reentered from the starboard wing. The dogs turned so slowly that any man could see that Chappel was arguing with himself, was forcing control; appealing to that formalistic and methodical self which had hauled him through so many scrapes. He entered the bridge, carefully dogged the hatch, turned and stood momentarily silent and dripping. His long face rose above the high collar of his waterproofs. The effect was of a man sired by experimental and equestrian gods. He backhanded water from his face, muttered, walked to the log, then hesitated above the entry. Chappel had logged ice, storm, death, and the loss of ships, but he had never logged a ghost.

"Unexplained weather phenomena, of no consequence." Levere's voice was pitched to serene authority that allowed no grand opinions. "Cutter *Able* is on fire. Give me *Abner's* position."

Chappel nodded as if the new information made complete sense. He wrote meticulously, then turned to the radio file and to his charts.

"I got the proceed-and-assist," said Howard. "I can't make *Abner's* send."

"That," said Chappel abstractly, "is the reason God made quartermasters." He turned to Howard. "You have not logged Wysczknowski to the bridge and to repair."

Howard turned, indignant.

"When your log is complete," said Levere, "raise *Aphrodite.* Then get on twenty mile range. I estimate another two hours."

"Watchstander?"

"Not unless you want to stand it," Chappel said. "I don't want to risk a man out there."

Howard, who in some vague way understood that he was taking flak because of the unknowable, and having perhaps been accused of being a Jonah, chose the course of wisdom and kept his big mouth shut.

"There is no excuse for a log to get behind," Levere said, "but the yeoman has been busy."

"I make it about twenty miles," Chappel told Levere, "assuming both ships maintained their direction of search since last position report."

Levere grunted above the crashing of waves, found a deep grunt at the top of a swell. The grunt expressed the opinion that, because it was *Able*, he was being asked to make a huge assumption. Howard hesitated between a sigh and a sneer, but he did not log the grunt.

XVII

~~~~~~

HOWARD WAS relieved from watch a half hour before *Adrian* closed *Aphrodite*, when *Aphrodite's* lights lay like a dusty glow on the horizon. Radioman James came to relieve the watch and assume his contact station. His natural, pale, meager remoteness was overlaid by a pallor like a man who, having vomited all but that last resource, had taken to vomiting blood. Howard looked at James, muttered to him that Chappel was raring to eat someone. Howard prepared to leave the bridge.

"How bad is it?" James whispered.

"You sick?"

"I'm never sick. Never. You know that."

"It's bad."

"They don't deserve that," James said. "It's a lousy ship, but nobody deserves that."

"I meant the other."

"The other isn't true." James spoke with firm conviction. "Levere logged weather, so it's weather. We all got to believe that."

"You weren't here."

"Has there been a situation report?"

"Static. All I can tell you is that they're still afloat."

Howard left the bridge and headed for the messdeck. He passed the galley where Lamp wedged his huge bulk in a corner and built cold ham sandwiches. On the messdeck, hands not on watch were assembled and ready to take station. Third engineman Masters, as lanky as Wysczknowski, but with a face like an elf's, looked up at Howard. He leered. Masters sat on the far, starboard side of the compartment. On some days, Masters appeared less grotesque than on others, or maybe it was that on some days he did not leer.

Men clustered on the damp, steaming messdeck. A few chewed on sandwiches, and the more adventurous attempted to drink rancid coffee from half-filled mugs; for even Lamp could not claim fresh coffee from that sea. *Adrian* rose in large and generous movements, coasting plumply down high, broad swells. The sea ran wide and huge. Shocks went through the ship each time it bottomed, and the half-full mugs spouted small brown geysers onto foul-weather gear that was already soaked.

Men stared at the coffee-splashed surfaces of tables. They muttered to each other, a half-dozen private conversations. They seemed a collection of broken parts—a watch cap pulled over one man's brows so that his eyes were dark sparks beneath the darker wool. An arm lay forward on a table, as if about to be chopped, the arm ending in a white clenched fist. Boots lay like dismembered feet, and a man's back arched in a questioning line as he bent and whispered to a fellow. A leg, Masters's, was contemptuously raised to plant a wet boot against a washed bulkhead, and streaks of dirty water ran down the clean white paint. Faces were halved by the huddled-together, half-dozen private conversations. There was no banter, no sarcasm, and men seemed to be isolating themselves from all but their most trusted chums. Brace, that nebulous part-time steward, part-time engineman, part-time seaman, sat alone and crouched, balled into himself in a far corner. He did not look like Amon, but he looked as Amon used to look just before crawling under a table.

Conally sat at the small table used by the bridge gang. Howard looked at Brace, then crossed the messdeck to sit with Conally. Footsteps sounded on the ladder and Glass appeared on the messdeck. He looked like he was casing a bank. He moved quietly to join Conally and Howard.

"Before you get started with your mouths," Glass said, "I just wanta say that Racca is your basic dirty guy. I get along with him, but that's what he is."

"How is he?" Howard was startled, having forgotten his patient.

"A lousy busted arm. We musta had ten busted arms on this ship."

"Well, ten busted somethings."

"All mouth," Glass said. "Did he break his mouth, we wouldn't be having this." Glass looked around the messdeck. He seemed like a citizen about to complain that you could never find a policeman when you wanted one.

"I ain't Lamp," Conally said, "but a guy can't help it if he gets to thinkin'."

"I've been on watch."

"Racca's passed the word," said Glass. "Racca claims the kid jonahed him into a bust arm, so the kid could get to the engine room."

"Brace wasn't anywhere near Racca."

"And Racca says it makes no difference. All a Jonah's got to do is be on board."

"These guys don't believe that. Nobody's that dumb." Howard looked about the messdeck as if he viewed the crew for the first time.

"No, but these guys are scared."

"A guy does get to thinkin'."

"You're a bosun's mate," Glass said, "you're not a pansy." Glass stood, a sort of passion of indignation driving him to his feet. "Going on deck," he said. "Up where the air's only fulla water." He could hardly have moved faster had he been making a getaway.

"I'd ought to book that punk," said Conally. "Only probably he's right." Conally seemed lost in thought or dream. "Lost that flyer, got that bumboat, and the steward sent crazy over Jensen. Busted arm, ghost on the mudflats, ghost ahead-a the ship, and Jensen talking in the fog . . . . " He stopped, looked at Howard, and Conally was a man who had tripped himself.

"He only grabbed me by the shoulder," Howard said. "It really happened."

"You sure?"

"I'm sure. I'm not Lamp, either. I know what happened."

"He said look out for ice." Conally looked around the mess-deck, bent forward like a conspirator. "Said, 'Ice—look out or you'll lose', an' that's all he said."

"You're sure it was Jensen?"

"Chum, do fish swim?"

Brace huddled, seemed entranced by Masters's dirty boot plunked against the bulkhead that Brace had scrubbed so many times. Brace's face was white with either fear or anger. As Conally and Howard watched, anger moved ahead of fear. A flush came to Brace's cheeks. His forehead wrinkled, and his eyes narrowed with the kind of joy men feel when they are about to beat one offender or another into the deck. Brace stood, his way blocked by men sitting at the table. He shook his head like a punchy hearing bells.

"Lemme past," he said. "I've had enough of this." He pushed the man next to him, and that man was Wysczknowski. Wysczknowski looked up, saw the flush across the pale face.

"You got a right to try," he told Brace, "but you try it on the end of a pier, not on this ship."

"Let the Jonah past," Masters said. "Let's see who can break what." He began to rise, but before he rose, he deliberately dragged the boot down the bulkhead.

Wysczknowski shook his head in a sort of sad amazement.

"You just made a nice piece of work for yourself, chum. When we pick up this tow, then you clean that mess. If you don't get it clean enough, you'll paint it."

Conally tapped Howard. "Get ready to get into this." The two men stood.

From forward a hatch boomed, a dog slammed and Dane's voice rumbled like engines. He called all hands to station. Conally and Howard stopped, paused, and Wysczknowski looked at Brace as if Brace was a circus poodle wearing a bow, a pink one. Brace stood in a futility of frustration as men reached for their gear and staggered forward to the ladder like soldiers making a stumbling attack across a plowed field. Brace looked at his clenched fists, caught his balance against a bulkhead, looked at the dark, dirty stain where Masters's foot had rested. He looked back at his fists as if they were pistols that had misfired. His fists unfolded into hands, and his hands trembled from a supply of adrenalin that had nowhere to go.

"I haven't got a station," he muttered to Wysczknowski. "I don't know who I'm working for."

"In that case you're working for me," Conally told him. "Get crackin'." Conally spun away and up the ladder. Howard headed for the medical locker. Brace followed, shrugging into his tarred and patched foul-weather jacket.

Aphrodite lay stern to the sea. A captain who had worked miracles in keeping the thing alive was working a little practical magic. With pumps meeting the leak, but not overcoming it, and with an engine running high and bearing a load for which it was not designed, *Aphrodite*'s crew of two deckhands and an engineman shifted everything moveable to starboard. The vessel's owner, who in later years would tire of buying senators and arrange to become one (his colleagues—having made their own arrangements—then calling him an honorable man), huddled life-jacketed and chattering in the wheelhouse, like a baboon that fears it will be robbed of a cookie.

The yacht lay head down as it backed into the swell. Floodlights cast nebulous pools to illuminate its narrow deck. The tall masts rose into darkness, and here and there, rigging that had been blown or cut away snapped, flapped, made near ghostly movements in the dark. The floodlights turned the surrounding sea blacker. The waterlogged bow was like a dull club as the thing slid into the trough. At each crash the bow dipped. Water swirled at the rails, crossed the forward deck beneath the lights in foaming currents, white, threatening, and eerie. Then, the reversing propeller extracted the bow from the sea as the stern lifted. The yacht heeled to starboard, and Howard, arriving on deck, did not at first see how that could reasonably be so.

"Runnin' on his port tank," Conally said. "Trying to shift weight to starboard so's to lift the leak."

"What's the word? Do we tow?"

"Pump if we can. Send a pump across. Maybe try to patch."

Floodlights along *Adrian's* deck and on the boat deck turned men into postlike figures of brilliance and shadow. The crew stood along the rail. From the darkened bridge shone the small glimmer of the chart light and the green glow from instruments. The radio threw static, blanked as Levere spoke to *Aphrodite*; then came static, and the clear answer from *Aphrodite*. Dane stood like a blot before the starboard running light, his head haloed in green. Brace stood beside Conally. He seemed both intimidated and defiant. Mutters from forward mentioned Brace. The mutters were deliberately pitched so that they could be heard along the rail, but not on the bridge. The sea rolled, dark, huge, cold and indifferent. Dane moved, disappeared into the dark bridge. A buzzer sounded from the engine room.

"Whatever we're going to do, we're doin' it," said Conally. He looked across the water at *Aphrodite*, at the churning white water washing the bow. Through the open hatch sounded the light, quick footsteps of Snow as he mounted the ladder from the engine room. Snow appeared on deck, tapped Wyszcknowski. "Relieve me on the board."

Wysczknowski moved, light and shadow, disappearing through the hatch like a man swallowed, gulped beneath a surface of steel.

"Boat crew," Dane bawled. "Get crackin'." He swung from the wing and stormed toward the boat deck.

Snow tapped Fallon. "Let us have a submersible and an engine to the boat deck."

"This is nuts," said Howard.

"Naw. Sea's high, but there ain't no wind, much." Conally hesitated, and it was certain that Conally did not know whether he spoke the truth or not. "Do me a favor. Get over there and fend off. Don't leave it to some other guy."

Fallon turned to Masters and McClean. "You heard the man."

"I heard," said Masters. "It's Jensen all over again."

McClean stepped forward, stepped back, finally got himself moving. "Lord, sweet Jesus. This one here's a pickle. This one here's a cob."

Masters stood and watched him go.

"You want a busted head," said Fallon.

"That's how this ship gets run. Always bustin' somebody." Masters moved, just fast enough that he could not exactly be criticized.

The red-headed Rodgers and bosun striker Joyce stood beside the small boat like convicts about to be hanged. Dane worked on the boat, stripping the cover, and Conally, arriving, stripped the stays. "Take the deck," he hollered at Joyce. "We're taking along some snipes."

Snow tapped Rodgers. "You stay aboard also, lad. The black gang must earn its living."

Fallon stepped forward.

"You are presently the senior engineer," Snow told him. "Stand down."

Fallon mumbled, looked relieved, looked guilty. Glass tumbled into the boat. Fallon turned to see McClean and Masters struggling forward with the gear. The boat was ready, and Dane, Conally and Glass sat hunched, hands steadying against the falls. Snow turned to Joyce. He pointed at McClean and Masters. "Which man is the better oar?"

Bosun striker Joyce blinked, nearly cringed. It was the first time his professional judgment had ever been consulted.

"They ain't neither of them amounts to a seaman, but I never saw Masters catch a crab."

"Nor ever will," said Masters. "Especially not tonight." He stood above Snow, edging sideways and managing to cringe from Dane at the same time. He half raised his hands in either protest or defense. "It's Jensen," he said, helpless, a near whine. "Jensen."

"I have no time to deal with you."

"I'll go." Brace stepped toward the boat, and he did not step timidly. He turned to face Snow. "I've got nothing going for me aboard this pig iron, anyway. Have I?" He swung back, climbed into the boat. "Get the gear up here." He leaned forward to hoist the pump, then the engine. "Later," he told Masters. "Your boot down your throat."

"If you girls is done gossiping," said Dane, and he began roaring. If Dane spoke words, no one understood them in an exact way, but in a general way they could have been understood as far off as Boston. Men tended lines. The boat lowered as Howard ran to the main deck and fended off. As the boat reached the rail, Snow spoke mildly to Dane, as though they were not about to set down on swells that ran towering above the bridge.

Adrian climbed the seas, rode the tops of swells, and then dropped with alarming speed into the troughs. The small boat hung like a white shiver of Joyce's fear as he took charge of the deck. To lower the boat at the bottom of the trough would splash it, rising faster than the ship. To lower at the top would allow the ship to run faster than the boat. Either maneuver could haul it beneath the swell, or throw it upward crashing into the davits. Joyce waited for the front side of a swell.

"Now."

"Unhooked forward."

"Unhooked aft."

"Hump it. Hump it."

Adrian rolled, seemed to devour the boat in shadow, and then the white flash of the thing escaped to stern, oars flailing like arms of the drowning.

Howard ran up the ladder, aft, watching the boat. He saw shapes of men leaving the boat deck. He nearly tripped over Joyce who half knelt against a chain.

"You did good," Howard told him.

"Just lea' me alone." Joyce made sounds in his throat, his belly. He leaned forward on hands and knees, vomiting.

"You need a hand?"

"I'll hose it down," Joyce said. "Only don't never tell nobody, willya."

Adrian worked to starboard as Levere came nearly cross sea to make a lee. The roll returned in a head-snapping shuffle down the swells that made the mast sing like a stringed instrument. The boat appeared, disappeared, appeared. The oars were steady. If Brace was pulling like supercargo, it could only be because he was intent on not crabbing his oar. Above the crash of water, Dane's voice set the stroke and made comments about potlickers.

Howard dusted at himself, like a man on the plains and not at sea. He had a watch list that needed revamping. He made his way to the bridge.

Chappel stood, horse-headed and silent. Levere stood on the port wing, while Majors spun the helm. Chappel looked at Howard. "I should not have spoken as I did, earlier. We'll discuss it later."

150

Radioman James looked at Howard, looked miserable. He motioned Howard to the wing.

"They got casualties," he said. "Two on *Able* and one on *Abner*. I don't hardly know what to say."

Howard stood, someplace between wonderment and fear.

"A' course, they won't say much on the box," James said. "Except—you know how you can read that Diamond?"

Howard nodded, dumb, and now truly in fear.

"Because he's a dago, probably," James explained. "Emotional." He paused. Helpless. "Two of them got bad burns on *Able*. Your friend Wilson . . . don't give it any hope, no hope a'tall. I read that Diamond's voice."

XVIII

~~~~~~

THAT FIRST, that original Jonah, sitting beneath wilted leaves in a drying wind and wondering what in the empty world to do next, could hardly have been more heartsick and confused than Howard who crept like a wounded man to the small sanctuary of his office. On his way across the messdeck he drew a mug of coffee, tasted the stuff, gagged. He emptied the mug and placed it in a rack.

Something definite had happened with the small boat. *Adrian* now ran head to sea, treading the high swell in a series of monotonous, crashing, engine-rumbling actions that seemed less sensible than the bobber on a fishline, no more sensible than empty rafts on an ocean. A few men clustered on the messdeck, sleepy from the long night, but huddling in the bright lights there rather than making the journey forward to the darkened crew's compartment. Howard made movement to unlash a chair, thought better of it, and sat on his small desk. He propped his back against a file cabinet and braced his feet against a bulkhead. He sat fore-and-aft in the dark office, easy with the pitch, defenseless against a roll.

Bastions of belief—as old men remember—are tough walled. A man trots easily through zoonomias of belieflessness. Though he may have the most demanding and silly faith, he is sound for as long as the bastion stays unbreached. Howard gagged, pushed at the bulkhead as if he tried to shove the ship apart. Lamp appeared in the hatchway bearing a steaming mug. Lamp seemed somehow old and foolish, a man who carried a mug but who projected no illusion.

"This is fresh," Lamp said. "I got a little teapot in the galley. Make a couple cups at a time." He passed it to Howard.

Howard, grateful, and unerringly knowing that he was in no shape to express it, sipped at the coffee and stared past the bulking, shadowed form of Lamp. He looked from the darkened office onto the brilliantly lighted messdeck.

"Wilson wasn't nosy enough to get killed," Howard said. "He wasn't even nosy enough to be a yeoman."

"This is the worst winter, this is the baddest winter I ever remember."

"It isn't even winter. It's October."

"November," Lamp told him. "We've passed over to November." He hesitated, was apologetic. "Did their radioman say how it happened?"

"They'd never allow that on the radio, ever." Howard sipped at the coffee, burned his mouth. "It's a carnival. That kid is right."

Lamp seemed ready to tell a story, to hark back to some miserable winter peopled with Chinamen, or to tales of wooden-hulled icebreakers parting the mists of Puget Sound. Then he thought better of it, standing in the hatchway with his back to the messdeck. He stared past Howard into the darkened wardroom. Lamp did not simply seem old. Lamp *was* old. The shock of that fact pressed Howard against the file cabinet in a

153

sort of spasm of disbelief as his legs pressured the bulkhead. Lamp was not as old as Dane, but he was certainly older than Snow. Without the mug, and without the hasty solicitude, Lamp no longer looked foolish. He was not the man that any other man would choose for a father, if a man could choose a father; yet the sireless Howard watched him and perhaps felt—if only a little—that a few foundations were untumbled.

Lamp seemed to be peering into a long tunnel of night. He stared into the wardroom, and his heavy bulk was supported against the pitch by outspread arms. Like an overweight crucifix, a stretched Buddha, he hovered on ancient steel plates entombed between sea and sky.

"We've had enough, Jensen," Lamp said. "If you had a job to do, you've done it."

Lamp touched Howard's knee. Pointed. Howard moved from his position, lost balance against the sea, regained his balance. He peered into the dark wardroom, and his eyes adjusted slowly after having looked at Lamp's dark silhouette against the bright lights of the messdeck.

The apparition, the dark dungarees in the small black vault of the wardroom, slumped headless, handless. Legs disappeared beneath the table where feet, if there were any, might extend through steel and be planted against the hull itself. The darkness of the apparition was a faint illumination on the deeper darkness of the wardroom. The figure sat, leaned forward as though it placed an invisible head on dungaree-covered arms lying crossed on the table. It sat motionless, like an exhausted man sleeping.

"The boys can't take no more," Lamp said. "This is your crew, chum."

Shoulders of the dungaree shirt raised, hunched, relaxed, raised, and it was clear that the figure wept. Sounds of weeping, or perhaps only sounds of the wash of the sea, echoed in the black chamber of the wardroom. Then fading, darkening, black merging into black—Jensen disappeared.

154

From behind Lamp, footsteps sounded in a hard pounding rush. The elfish, and frightened, and certainly guilty face of Masters appeared like a hiss of hysteria.

"Who are you talking to? What is it?" Masters shouldered his way past Lamp, stood looking at Howard, then turned to Lamp.

"He was talking to me," Howard said, "and this office is off limits to punks."

Masters stood in the darkened office, his guilt changing to desperate despair. "A quill driver," he said, "and a fat cook. You lie like rugs."

Lamp reached with one foot to kick away the curving brass hook that secured the door. He closed the door carefully, like a man determined not to break anything. He twisted the worn, black light-switch and the office was illuminated. Howard backed toward the wardroom, dropped the mug, heard it smash. Howard was not a little frightened. Howard, and possibly no other man, had ever seen Lamp behave as Lamp behaved. Masters was not less than six feet, weighed not less than one-hundred-seventy, and yet, when Lamp leaned forward to snatch him by the belt and raise him into a corner of the office, Masters seemed like a small rag doll.

"You yellowed on the boat deck," Lamp told him. "You're tryin' to start something." He gave Masters a shake, and Masters's head bonged against the angle formed by bulkhead and overhead. "Ain't you? Ain't you?"

Masters gasped, tried to arch backward, either to kick, or to relieve pressure from the belt that was cutting beneath his small ribs, chewing at his kidneys.

"Because if you *can* start something," Lamp said, and he rattled Masters against the bulkhead, "if you can get everybody scared, then the boys will forget you're yellow."

"He's about to get hurt bad," Howard said timidly. "It's breaking his back."

Lamp's forearm trembled. His voice lowered. He gave Masters a shake that rattled Masters's head into the corner with a beat as steady as a fighter on a bag.

"I don't book guys," Lamp told Masters. "And I don't threaten them. This here's a promise."

Masters choked, looked like he was dying.

"One word. One. There ain't a place *far* enough, or a hole *deep* enough, that I can't find you. Got that? Have you got that?"

Masters choked and gulped, tried to nod his banging head.

"Okay. Out." Lamp dropped Masters, and Masters thumped gasping into the corner.

"And take the word to Racca," Lamp told him. "Does he want something busted besides his arm?"

Lamp shrugged, turned toward Howard in a nearly placid manner. He was like a man easy in his mind after making a small and successful decision. "I got this bad temper," he said apologetically. "Had to fight it pretty much all my life."

Howard, who was mildly democratic, and who would have sworn that he could deal with reality, felt that the world which he thought he understood had just turned fish-belly up. "I better pick up these pieces," he said apologetically. He began to kneel to get the broken mug.

Adrian skidded, kept skidding, kept skidding, to end with a thump that bent hinged knees and threw Lamp and Howard into squats. Masters, feeling his way to his feet, was knocked backward. He fell. Masters banged an already well-banged head.

"Where did that come from?"

"Count seven."

Adrian ran another swell, banged hard, but it did not run the long line of travel that accompanied the first swell.

"That's one."

On the seventh swell, *Adrian* skidded, skidded, kept skidding, skidding, and the jolt rattled tables that were welded to the deck in wardroom and messdeck.

"It's a new storm," Lamp said. "Or the other one moved in a circle."

"No wind."

"It's out there someplace."

"If it's circling."

"It may find us. Maybe not."

Masters managed to stand. He did not exactly look chastened, but he looked like a man with a brand new way of viewing matters. "We got guys aboard that scow." He propped himself against a bulkhead, flapped one hand, helpless, turned to the hatch. He fled with all the dignity he could muster, about the same dignity owned by a mired donkey.

"At least you stopped him talking."

"Naw," Lamp said. "He'll talk. He just won't talk as loud."

"What do you make . . . ?" Howard pointed to the darkened wardroom.

"It's a sign," Lamp said easily. "What we got to do is figure out the sign."

Howard had lost count. He thought the next wave might be the seventh. He steadied himself. "You weren't afraid." The wave was the seventh. *Adrian* roller-coastered, thumped, crashed.

"Nothing to be scared about," Lamp said. "Jensen was a shipmate." Lamp prepared to leave. "I got to figure some way to get these guys some coffee. I got to get something in some bellies." He was suddenly a man ridden by anxiety, like a high school boy dared by his pals into a date with an older and experienced woman. He seemed ready to bustle, to explain legends, to become, in fact, the Lamp whom Howard had known for so long.

"Don't you ever sleep?"

"Does Levere?"

Howard was about to say that it was not the same. "I guess I ought to check Racca," he said. "Then go to the bridge. We're in for it."

Lamp flapped one hand, helplessly. "I've lost friends," he said. "I'm awful sorry about your friend Wilson." Then he fled, a man chased by abstract demons of memory which now wore the mild and practical names of hot cereal and fresh coffee.

In the hours before dawn the temperature plummeted; Howard, headed forward, stepped to the main deck to lean against a chain with both hands. The cold steel, the freezing air, and wisps of spray thrown from forward by the bow helped wake him. He stared into the dark sea that ran alongside, and he stood spraddle-legged against the increasing pitch. Phosphoresence spun past the hull in thin flashes like schools of fish. He tested for wind, found none except the small breeze raised by *Adrian*'s passage. In the scuppers, water ran from the breaking bow-wave, and, along the edges of the scuppers, mushy salty-water ice formed a thin line, a promise, a threat; the line like a pencil of definition running the circumference of the ship.

Forward and to starboard, no more than a half mile distant, *Aphrodite* glowed against the dark sky and darker sea. Men were clustered forward. In the bright floodlights powered by a portable generator, the men moved like a congregation of shadows, as water washed across the sagging bow. They were like creatures of surf, primal; forms rising from the immense tide pool of the sea. Alongside *Aphrodite* the small boat bounced, was fended off by three, or possibly four, dark figures. The small boat moved alongside *Aphrodite*'s hull, and the figures bent over a bulky lump from which lines radiated to the deck.

Dane was attempting to rig a sea patch. Dane was not fooling around by casting the thing on the breath of a little hope, a little prayer. As Howard watched, *Aphrodite* turned its stern two points across the sea to press rushing water against the hull. The patch went over, the lines straightened, and the boat closed against the pitching yacht. For minutes Howard stood, leaning against the chain, mute. Then, from a distance, he heard shouting. He pushed himself erect, ready for action, a jolt of fear urging his feet toward the bridge. Then he stopped. The shouts were cheers. The wide mouth of the leak had sucked the patch.

"We've got it," Howard said. "They did it, chum. They did it, Wilson." He hesitated, looking up and down the deck as if he expected a reply. The only sounds were the sea, the distant hum of the generator, and the faint and distant voice of Dane hollering commands.

XIX

~~~~~~

"WE THOUGHT we'd lost that kid, boys. We were sure of it." Or so, in later years when cooking at the Base, Lamp would aver. By then, Lamp's huge arms were thinner. Sagging laps of flesh hung from his upper arms in that way of formerly robust women who have spent their lives among small cares, small hopes and large ambitions for others—and, of course, in company with brushes and laundry.

"Maybe you should of lost him, cook. Maybe you shoulda." Always a young voice would say that. Always an older voice would snort with contempt, or would curse.

Mother Lamp, who cherished increasingly the wayward souls of seamen, would bustle and tsk and wait until the smart-mouth had tacked his short nail of wisdom through the wide, implied fabric of the tale.

"It wasn't that way, sonny. You're listenin' with your mouth."

"He's a red-blooded American punk, cook. Don't pay him any mind."

"Brace was only a kid, himself," Lamp would say. "For awhile there he was a goner."

In that large galley, where assistant cooks and stewards ragged and nagged apprentices with dull chores, Lamp was like the director of a small and competent theater. In the waning days of his usefulness, and with indifference to the ambitions of lesser men who contrived to gain his excellent, shore-going job, it was Lamp's great luxury to sit garrulous on the messdeck—or, gaze silent, as if he still watched the crash of seas, like a man staring with serene indifference at memory, or at that black gulf which lies beyond all seas.

"The real miracle was," he would say, "that wind never found us. And it was huntin'. That kid was trapped for days." Which was, in the creative scope of Lamp's memory, the truth; although it did not precisely match the facts.

The facts, reconstructed after Howard ran like a skein of snoopiness through memory, the log, and conversations, were largely unornamental and bland.

In sloshing water beneath the dull glow of emergency lanterns, *Adrian's* boarding crew flattened and shored the sea patch aboard *Aphrodite*. Brace worked at the task of rigging the pump. The compartment was narrow, awash, dark. It was certainly a dungeon when Brace became pinned shoulder deep in water beneath a shifting, tangled mire of gear.

"Like Floyd Collins, boys. Stuck at the bottom of a mine."

In those shadowed days when the world was still fabulous, before the rise of clans and explanations; before, even, the invention of hulls, the trapped Brace would have been the stuff of legends, of myth, of song. Before the race became old with knowledge, and thus voluntarily stupid, Brace would have courted and won a place among heroic tales told before dying fires. But . . . in fact, he was only a terribly frightened youngster who was trapped in the forward compartment of *Aphrodite*.

"Scared crazy," Glass told Howard on the following day as *Adrian* steamed slowly toward Boston, escorting *Aphrodite* which still ran heeled to port. "Of drowning. Dane smacked him around some."

"We were all scared crazy," Howard said, and he seemed to be hearing echoes. "Brace's name came up in conversation."

"Snow finally got him quiet," Glass said. "It took an hour to cut him loose."

"It was a tough hour aboard this ship."

The tough hour began when yeoman Howard, having seen the patch set into the heavy suction of the leak aboard *Aphrodite*, and having spoken honorably and well to Wilson, turned from the thinly iced main deck toward the after hatch. Above him on the boat deck the small sounds of a man working were as unconcerned and unapologetic as the movement of mice. Then the sounds stopped as the man realized that someone else was present. The pale face of bosun striker Joyce looked down, saw Howard, and Joyce released a huff of frozen breath. He steadied himself against a chain. *Adrian* swooped down a long swell.

"You come topside for a minute?" Joyce's voice seemed more frozen, less mobile than his breath.

Howard walked aft, mounted the after ladder and moved across the familiar deck. He was arrested by a lifeline.

"In case the weather gets back up," Joyce said.

"You need help?"

"I already got the fantail rigged." Joyce pulled a wool mitten from one hand with his teeth, mumbled, used the freed hand to throw a turn and two half-hitches. He looked like he was trying to warm his tongue. He mumbled, retrieved the mitten, pulled it back onto his hand. "Levere ought to know," he said. "This whole ship's awake. Guys are talking." He leaned on the line, jogged it, grabbed with mittened hands to rock back and forth with all his weight to test the line. "I don't need help," he said apologetically. He looked at the dark sea, turned to look forward, looked upward where the masthead floated and tipped, as though the mast were a string that danced and dangled the puppet ship *Adrian*.

"Racca claims he's got the gangrene," Joyce said.

"In his head. That was a clean break."

"I wish Dane was here. I wish Snow was." Joyce gave a final bounce against the line. "I don't want to be on deck with Jensen around," he said, "and I don't want to go below. Racca's crazy."

"I was scared," Howard told him. "Then Lamp said something. This is Jensen's crew. Jensen wouldn't do anything to hurt this crew."

The mast tipped forward like an ancient weapon wielded to exorcise demons. Water fountained from the bow, white flowers of foam. The stack rumbled as positive as an introit. "I never thought of that," Joyce said. "That's good. You can't be scared when you think that." He twanged the taut line, grabbed it to enjoy the vibration through the mitten. For a moment he was nearly jubilant. Then, a man struck by an awareness of situation, he became a mourner. "Everybody's sorry about Wilson," he said. "Everybody's talking."

"I'm not." Howard, who was occasionally known to have a happy fight with French or English sailors, looked down at his clenched fists. "This time," he said, "this time you can find out who to kill."

"Guys say Wilson is what the sign was about." Joyce paused, for a moment at least, in the presence of murderous intent. "Maybe Wilson made a mistake," he murmured. "He maybe did it to himself."

"He was a country boy," said Howard, "but he wasn't that much of a country boy."

"Not me," said Joyce. "I'm from Philadelphia."

"Let's get below. Get warm."

Joyce twanged the line. He looked aft at the wake tossed and spread by the sea. He mumbled.

"You coming below?" Howard turned, walked toward the after ladder.

"Howard."

"Yes."

"I know what you mean about Philadelphia. But it's home, sorta. A guy can't help where home is."

Ice lay in the cleats of the ladder. Thin silverings of ice lay on the taut lifelines stretched across the fantail. Howard went through the after hatch, crossed the fiddley and looked down to see McClean standing on the plates. Fallon stood at the board. His keglike shape was grouped into itself, like a caged bear held by invisible bars. Fallon looked up, saw Howard, motioned with a thick hand. McClean saw Fallon's motion, looked up into the darkness of the fiddley. McClean stood in the bright lights of the engine room like a tired man pinned to a landscape by intense sunlight. His nearly tan face was sweaty from engine heat and seemed radiant with light and sweat.

Howard fumbled down the always almost-slick ladder. He arrived on the plates.

"Lamp did a number on Masters," Fallon said. "You were there."

"He had it coming." Howard was surprised. "Guys on the messdeck heard it?"

"A mouse can't poot aboard this ship without." McClean stood easily on the plates, and his weight moved with the forward-running, wave-smacking motion of *Adrian*. "Masters ain't going to 'fess getting licked by a cook."

"Last thing Lamp ever licked was a spoon."

"You weren't there," Howard told Fallon. "Lamp swabbed the deck with that guy."

Fallon looked like he was trying to spell a tough word. "Maybe the kid. When Amon left, Lamp adopted the kid, sort of." Fallon looked at the board, reached to make a minor adjustment on a valve. His arm was thick, tattooed with a clumsy, unsinuous picture of a woman. Beneath that tattoo was another, the traditional fouled anchor.

"He was taking care of the ship," Howard said. "Guys were afraid."

"Guys *are* afraid."

164

"Lamp said something." Howard explained. " . . . Jensen . . . his crew, after all . . . wouldn't do anything to hurt this crew."

"Now there's a relief," McClean said. "That there is a bonified relief."

"Tell the guys up forward," said Fallon. "When you think like that, you can't get scared."

"Lamp says it's a sign."

"I never paid much attention to that cook. Y'know, that's a pretty good cook."

Howard climbed from the engine room, stood on the grates and looked down into the brilliantly lighted space. The whooshing updraft of hot air and the rumble of the engines blanked the wash of the sea. McClean and Fallon stood unmasked as themselves. There was no illusion, no suggestion of Jensen on those plates. One sign seemed clear. Jensen did not want Brace in the engine room. Jensen seemed to be a jealous lesser spirit in the land of a jealous god.

Forward and to port was the crew's compartment. Howard slowly descended the ladder. A man sat against the lower step of the ladder. He appeared as a dark bulk beneath the red glow of dull nightlights. The ancient hull of *Adrian* creaked, rattled; the old steel still firm along the welds but growing infirm across featureless steel plates stretched between points of stress. Water that had been carried to the deck on boots lay in a thin, red sheen. The red lights toned the edges of shadow, and it intensified the darkness of shaded bunks and corners. The crew's compartment was not musty, as it would have been if men were sleeping. The smell, if it was a smell, telegraphed anxiety, and a sense of pending combat.

The man who sat against the bottom step was hunched over, dark, stolid, and he did not turn as Howard descended the ladder. A few feet forward, and starboard in the compartment, the redhead Rodgers sat beneath a red light. He wedged between a bulkhead and a locker. Rodgers whistled thinly, and he seemed pleased with his innovation. He looked forward and to port, where midships in the compartment lay the dark form of Racca stretched on a bunk. Beside the bunk, and directly beneath a light, Masters stood like a Samaritan elf about to spread ointment or unction. Bosun striker Joyce, having preceded Howard, sat on a bottom bunk and watched the whistling Rodgers. Joyce's wet mittens lay in two small piles beside him, dark and steaming as venial sins. Joyce held a swab in one hand, and he pushed it back and forth across the area of deck he could reach without standing. *Adrian* pitched, rose to a high swell.

Howard squeezed against a rail to pass the sitting man. It was Wysczknowski, and Wysczknowski looked at Howard, his tight-lipped Polack face a warning against abrupt movement.

"Is it about anything," Wysczknowski said, "or are you another one asking for a rap in the chops?"

Elfin Masters looked up, saw Howard, reached to tap the woozy Racca on his foot. Racca, like a man rehearsed, moaned, gave a small yelp, a creak like worn steel plates. Racca's uninjured arm flopped. His hand rose and groped in the space between two bunks. The hand floated pale and redly washed. Racca looked like he offered a blessing.

Howard took a chance. "Are you all nuts?" he said to Wysczknowski.

"Them two," Wysczknowski said and pointed at Masters and Racca. "I ain't sure about them others."

"I keep trying to tell you something," Joyce said. "You guys won't listen."

Rodgers whistled a slow march tune, learned, no doubt, at his high school graduation. He fumbled at his shirtfront, a man confusedly caught without a crucifix. Racca moaned, raised his uninjured arm. He pointed forward. His arm trembled, shook, pounded the air. It was galvanic, like Amon's seizure.

Masters looked elfishly at Howard and Wysczknowski. In the red lights his twisted face was leering. He was a man showing off. He was showing what he could do.

"Lamp whipped him for being yellow," Howard said. "He figures Lamp won't do it if he's crazy."

"He's crazy." Wysczknowski sat unmoving, but prepared. "We got enough trouble. Levere has got enough trouble."

Howard, who had not heard about the trapped Brace, listened while Wysczknowski explained.

"Dane is there."

"And Snow. They say we're going to Boston."

Masters leered. He passed a hand in front of Racca's face. He hissed.

"Brace," Racca moaned. Then in clear and somber tones he pontificated. His voice sounded like he was a senator praising soybeans.

"Brace is off the ship," Racca proclaimed. "Brace must stay off the ship."

Masters raised his elfin face into the red light like a satanic worshipper engaged in foul prayer.

"Brace," he hissed. "Jensen."

Racca pointed.

"There they are," said Racca, in the wise and pontifical tones. "Brace and Jensen have returned to the ship. Please do not hurt us, Brace. Please do not hurt us, Jensen."

His pontifical tone faded, he whimpered, choked like a man dying. "Don't touch me—oh there . . . there . . . there . . . they are!"

"There—there—there—they—are!" Masters twirled slowly in the red light, the light chasing after the crevices and lines of Masters's face. He did an eternally slow pirouette. He stopped and faced forward.

"I don't want to go with you," he said. His voice rose in a low shriek. "Leading me, he's leading me, he's come for me . . . . " Masters blubbered, wept, recoiled against Racca's bunk. He held to the frame of the bunk. His body was pulled, snatched, pressed backward as if invisible hands were dragging him. His elf face seemed to pull upward into his forehead, the diamond-shaped chin was lost in shadow as he ducked his head. Slobber fell like a sprinkle of blood onto the red, wet deck. Then Masters dived to the deck as if he chased his own blood. He lay flat, and his eyes were wide and unseeing. His slightly bowed arms shook, began to knock toward each other, and he fell forward again and started to writhe and flop as if jolted with electricity. His hands clawed at the deck. Then his body was thrust sharply upward, sideways, flopped back. Masters looked like he was being kicked by invisible feet.

"They've come," moaned Racca.

"Don't—oh—don't—don't—hurt." Masters's body was thrown in the other direction. It was nearly impossible to believe that he was not being kicked.

"Is he puttin' on?"

"I don't know." Howard's voice was awed.

Masters scrabbled about the deck like a crab. Masters vomited bile. Masters's corpselike eyes stared, stared.

Rodgers stood and went to sit in quick companionship beside Joyce. Joyce looked up, jumped, looked forward where the figure of a man slowly rolled out of a bunk. Howard followed Joyce's frightened stare with a frightened stare of his own. He waited for the worst.

The figure was leaned over the bunk, feeling beneath the pad. Hands appeared and the hands were holding a pack of smokes. The figure lit a cigarette, then turned toward the light. Gunner Majors shook himself like a dog shaking down its fur.

"You punks won't let a man sleep," he mourned. "You just keep at it and keep at it. Don't I have enough trouble with wet guns?" He dragged at the cigarette, stepped to the forward bulkhead for a CO_2 extinguisher. Masters flopped and slathered and gurgled. He began to make crablike movements toward the ladder. Wysczknowski stood.

Majors flipped the cigarette to the deck, toward Masters's legs.

"We got a fire," Majors said. "You see it there." He spoke in calm tones of disgust. He pointed at the cigarette. Then he stripped the seal of the extinguisher and pulled the pin. He pointed the extinguisher at the deck. Gas exploded with a roar. It boiled, foamed, expanded; even the sea crashing against the hull was cloaked and silenced by the roar. The gas coiled from the deck no more than six feet from Masters's crotch. Frost formed on Masters's boots. Oxygen disappeared. Men put their arms over their faces, sucked hard to breathe.

Majors stopped. He waited for the cold ice mist to dissipate. He viewed his handiwork.

Masters sat up. He held his hands over cold testicles.

"There's just one word for you, Majors," said Masters. "You're a bastard." The elf face was contorted with indignation.

"Bastard," echoed Racca. "Bastard—bastard—bastard—come to save us—"

Majors squeezed the trigger of the fire extinguisher. A burst of gas choked its way toward Masters. Masters flipped over on his face. Then he scrambled to his feet.

"Bastard," Racca moaned. "Oh, save us, bastard, save us."

"Shut up," Masters told Racca. "Before I bust your other arm." He stood beneath the red lights, and, like McClean and Fallon who had stood on the plates, Masters was unmasked. He was only himself, trembling, perhaps doing his best to control compulsions of fear or guilt.

"If I don't get some sleep, I'm gonna die." Majors checked the pressure gauge on the extinguisher, thinking, perhaps, that he would have to alibi to get it recharged.

"Climb into your sack," Majors told Masters, "or do I get the handcuffs?"

"He was acting." Wysczknowski shook his head in pure wonderment. "It was an act."

"We'll know when we get to Boston." Howard turned to Majors. "He really under arrest?"

"I'm master at arms, and I need sleep—so, yeah, he's under arrest." He turned back to Masters. "Get out of that sack for any reason, any, and you get locked in with the hawser."

"You want me to log it?"

"I'll be up there in a minute," Majors said. He turned back to Masters. "If we got us a Jonah, boy, then I know who."

When Howard arrived on the bridge, radioman James leaned against the set like a wisp of paleness and fatigue. His frailty, no matter his protests, would always sooner or later hunt him to ground.

"I'll take it for awhile," said Howard. "I'll call you for important traffic."

"The generator burned on *Able*," James told him. "That's the only thing we've heard that's new."

"It's history. Lay below."

"I'm okay."

"Nobody said you weren't. Lamp said there was going to be fresh coffee."

"Just the trick. That's just the trick." James read the routine for turning over the watch. He looked out at the flaring lights of *Aphrodite*.

"If we don't get wind."

"Dane's there."

"Fresh coffee. Just the trick." James disappeared down the ladder like a puff of mist.

Howard checked the radar screen, flicked between ranges, adjusted the set. If a storm was batting around, it was still not on the screen.

The radio blanked as a transmitter opened nearby. The silly-sounding voice of a man hollered: "How soon? When? Hurry up. How soon?"

"The guy who owns the boat," said Chappel. "He keeps doing that. Wants to be taken off."

"Remind him of procedure," said Levere. "This time tell him we have the power of arrest."

"I didn't know that, cap."

"We don't," said Levere. "When we get done with this, you must read up on the law."

The radio blanked, as the transmitter again opened aboard *Aphrodite*. "Get outta the way," said Glass, "or you get a knuckle sandwich." Glass's voice was tense, either with situation or with the intent to back up a promise. "Cap," said Glass, "we got him loose and he ain't hurt."

Levere sat immobile. Silent and silhouetted like a man finishing a prayer. "Tell Glass to follow procedure," he said. "I want to speak to *Aphrodite*'s master." He slouched in the captain's chair, and his fatigue, which never showed, now seemed to be pressing him toward the deck. He waited until the radio spoke with the voice of his friend.

"Can you steam, Tom?"

"We can. Slowly."

"I'll leave two men aboard you," said Levere. "Let's head for the barn."

Dane stayed aboard *Aphrodite*, and Dane kept Brace with him. *Aphrodite* and *Adrian* went to Boston, at three knots, where upon arriving, *Aphrodite*'s owner fired *Aphrodite*'s captain and attempted to pick up his master's papers with a charge of incompetency. A carbon of a complaint arrived for Levere. It charged Levere with hazarding life at sea, and it charged *Adrian*'s crew with the theft of a piece of canvas; and, yeoman Howard, with a hard-mouthed determination to track down injustice, discovered that history is rigged so that you can never find out who to kill.

XX

THESE ARE the bars of Scollay Square, adrift with crud, busted wine bottles, trash, garbage, and huddled lumps of decaying clothing which swaddle passed-out flesh that dries and dies in doorways beneath the benison of those Irish idealists, worn with cocky servitude into creatures of fists: the police.

Streets wind downhill to the moorings where masts cluster like burned forests, and where museum ships bearing proud names and bold history endure fossilized protection; as schoolchildren—and less able tourists—stick chewing gum beneath the rails as they touristly gossip with proprietary smugness of revolutions made by others.

Cutter *Able* lies burned and scorched in dry dock. Cutter *Adrian* hangs at the pier, aflash with the quick, hot torches of welders; as workmen rapidly cut, add, patch, and get the thing ready in all respects to return to sea. Cutter *Abner*, en route to stand by for *Able* in New Bedford, is apprised that the overdue

Seascamp was never lost. A change of plans, unreported, took it to New York where, it is rumored, politely ladled measures of gin and scotch cloud all thought of possible error, even through the longest and darkest hours of night.

"F'I had a deed to all the real estate in this town that I've puked on, I'd be a rich an' happy man."

These bars of Scollay Square. Men take their first drinks and vow to proceed to the yid district where seaman Glass has "connections." The men drink one, drink another against the journey. Through frosted windows they watch dull streets. Yellow stains of nicotine cover the panes to slump with running drops of thaw in spots where hot blasts from chugging ceiling furnaces loosen filth that runs like the yellow track of a portentous, sniffing, leg-raising hound. Women, on their last downhill leg—women born unlucky, or charmed, and certainly born unto ignorance, that one true mark of Cain—the women laugh, go haw-haw; pretend that at some time during their lives they have been happy for longer than fifteen consecutive minutes. Young sailors look at the ham-handed, billy-club-packing bartenders. The sailors rub the lips of beer glasses with the palms of their hands. They pretend to be thinking, as they superstitiously rub beer on the glass in hope of killing germs that pack rare disease.

"Don't get cranked up here," Glass told Brace. "They'll roll you for your socks."

"Why'd we come here, then?"

"It's in every guidebook," Howard told him. "Always visit the Chamber of Commerce first."

"You used to be a funny guy."

"I don't feel funny anymore."

The men drink a third beer, then a fourth, in preparation for the cold trip crosstown.

"I wish I could meet a decent woman."

Howard, who has learned the great secret, and who, after beer, is generous: "Go to a library."

"You yeomen is all alike."

"It's true," said Howard. "Two thirds of all sailers who marry meet their wives in libraries"—a statistical exaggeration by Howard, who, doing correct calculation, would have arrived at only half that figure.

"Makes sense, sorta. Where else can a decent woman be seen talkin' to you?"

The men drink a fifth beer, a sixth.

Brace looked through the windows at the cold streets. He was reluctant to move into that darkness, and the reluctance showed on the once bland face that was now creased here and there with a light wrinkle. He looked around the seamy, grungy, spit-ridden bar. His movements, once quick and inaccurate, were now deliberate. He whirled his flat hat on one finger.

"It's either about something," he said, "or it isn't. I'm going back to the ship."

Howard stood. "I'll come with."

Glass stood. "Me, too. If I did go over that way, I'd probably just run into my folks."

"Because things are changing," said Brace. "Everything is changing."

Some change was abrupt. Racca and Masters left the ship, Racca on a stretcher and Masters escorted by Majors. Three days later, as the first heavy snow swirled between buildings and danced in a northeast declamation along the pier, Racca returned with his arm in a cast. The snow slopped along brick streets where traffic churned dirt, mixing the snow into a cold custard of filth. As the wind increased, and the snow increased, ships along the pier faded. The white bows melted into wind and snow, and the ships became spectral blots of white on white.

Racca smiled, gossiped, grinned. He clowned. He was a juggler of his emotions, a bare adept who managed not to weep. McClean helped pack Racca's gear. Men who did not even like Racca, much, pretended that he would soon return to limited duty, but it was clear that Racca was ashore to stay.

Masters pretended madness, and was believed. The first storm died. The second storm moved in with an immense burden of snow, as if the storm attempted to cloud and hide the shame of the dirty streets. Masters talked and talked and talked; to doctors, and to a legal officer. He accepted a general discharge.

"He got off easy," said Glass. "They could of hung him high."

"This way causes less stink," Howard told him. "Plus, it's cheaper."

"Of course, if he's really crazy . . . "

Wysczknowski, dealing a perennial hand of solitaire, shifted uncomfortably. The messdeck, where Brace mopped, was constantly damp with melted snow. The ship was vaguely cold, and frosted breath combined with melted snow to cover bulkheads with a thin glaze of moisture that was not cold enough to freeze, not warm enough to evaporate. "Everybody was crazy," said Wysczknowski. "Masters yellowed out. The crazy part don't matter."

Some of the changes looked good. Fireman Schmidt transferred in from a weather cutter. Schmidt's square kraut head, with its regulation dress blue weather-cutter haircut, bent like a lover in the engine room, and it was clear that Schmidt was going to be okay.

Third engineman Bascomb, with a Georgia accent, transferred in from a buoy snatcher. Bascomb was a lanky, cracker-looking yahoo with a loud mouth who—according to scuttlebutt—got that loud mouth because, where he was raised, it was a far piece between the house and the barn. Men idly worried, watched Bascomb and McClean; were relieved when the two went ashore drinking, to return in a maudlin, foul-mouthed state, because bartenders were prejudiced against southerners.

Other change was subtle, and perhaps it was not change at all. Howard knew that Levere spent too much time in operations. Howard counseled himself with a dozen troubled speculations, chief among them the cold suspicion that either *Abner* or *Adrian* would be permanently assigned to New Bedford. Howard kept his silence against the awful day when the news would arrive, but the news did not arrive; and Howard, for two days, was otherwise occupied. When he could finally contrive no good official reason for calling *Abner*, he dug in his own pockets and looked for a pay phone. He hunched in his peacoat, shivering, frozen because he was ashore in a regulation, dress blues town. He dialed.

"Nobody here is talking," he said to radioman Diamond.

"It happened so fast," Diamond told Howard. "It's snowing hard here."

"We already have it here. Radio says they have it deep up home."

"I know," said Diamond. "I'm the radioman."

Yeoman Wilson, climbing from *Abner*'s small boat to the deck of *Able* while carrying a medical kit, had grabbed a chain. The chain gave way. Wilson fell backward, struck his head on the gunnel of the boat, and was dead.

"The hook had rusted," Diamond said. "Somebody tied that thing in place with marlin."

"A bosun's mate, then, or a seaman."

"Try to find out—you can't. Our guys already been that route."

"There's a board of investigation."

"They'll hang the captain," Diamond said, "and probably the chief bosun."

176

"But who really did it?"

"Try to find out—because no one knows. Maybe not even the guy who did it."

Some change only threatened.

"I want out of this," said Brace. "Where is that guy, Iris?"

Lamp, surrounded by the enormous port of Boston, thus with a surfeit of sinners, stayed aboard. His excellent cooking improved. While the rest of the crew forgot Jensen, and as Racca and Masters vanished more surely than spirits from their places on the messdeck, Lamp attacked the invisible. This time his attack was subtle, in the form of constant small surprises. Men peered suspiciously at silly desserts, at pink cupcakes—at creampuffs—which they licked experimentally, then wolfed. On the cold ship the only warm place was the galley, and steam from Lamp's fires spilled from the galley and clouded the messdeck. Brace mopped, squeegeed, swabbed, could not get rid of water.

"Iris is at the base in South Portland," Howard told Brace. "Waiting for us to get in."

"Quit complaining, sonny," Lamp told Brace. "We got November off. You want to be steaming in that mess out there?"

"Nobody's steaming, anyway."

Which was nearly true. During November, cutter *Aaron*, of Boston, towed fishing vessel *Pearl*. Cutter *Abner*, standby in New Bedford, towed fishing vessel *Stella*. Two men were reported in the surf at Hampton Beach. Dune pounders searched, recovered no one. As storms swept off the North Atlantic, traffic dropped. Fishermen doubled up their moorings, mended nets.

Brace complained, but his work improved. For the first time, Brace seemed to listen to his own complaint, hear his own voice. The tenor of complaint and voice changed. Brace seemed nearly reasonable; stoic, the victim trapped in a dentist's chair from which, sooner or later, he could step away drilled and patched and forgetful.

"A guy gets tired," he told Howard. "I don't mean the work, I mean the *kind* of work."

"You'll be out of it soon."

"I want to talk to you," Brace said covertly. "But not on the ship. You can't scratch your own can aboard this ship without it gets logged."

"It's not that bad."

"Maybe not," Brace said with a sincere attempt to speak justly, "but I want to talk off the ship."

The matter being perhaps serious, and Howard nosy, the two men met over five-cent cups of coffee in a run-down cafeteria where old men chewed, burped, scratched their crotches and looked at walls decorated with fading murals of sea battles between tall ships. Dim battle flags flew above washed-out spouts of cannon smoke that fumed beneath gray bulges of burning sails. A portrait purporting to be Nelson, or Farragut, or possibly the man who originally opened the cafeteria, hung above the cash register.

"I've been to this town four different times," Howard said. "I still haven't seen an admiral."

"You have to guess they're around somewhere." Brace leaned forward, elbows on the table, and the two white stripes of his apprenticeship seemed the only part of himself or his outfit that glowed. His regrown shock of undistinguished hair rode like an insipid layer of paint above a face that, to Howard, seemed mightily changed. Howard, himself nearly stilled by loss, and the awfulness of chance, and by fear, could only guess that Brace still thought of a dark, entrapping compartment where water reached toward his mouth.

"Is that true about libraries?"

"It's true."

"It's a good thing to know," said Brace, "but it's not what I want to talk about." He fumbled in his jumper, apologetically drew out a pack of smokes. Lit one. Offered one. "I don't want to go to the engine room. I don't want Levere to know that."

"Why tell me?"

"You're the guy does watch lists."

"That doesn't have anything to do with this."

"Okay," said Brace, "it doesn't. You're the guy who watches everything."

"You got cured of engine rooms?"

"I was scared," said Brace. "I can go belowdecks, but I don't like it any more. I don't like Dane all that much, but I don't like belowdecks."

"Dane's okay."

"I honestly don't know," Brace said. "He's different now. He's actually the one who got me loose."

"And he smacked you around."

Brace looked like a man who remembers the tenderness of romance long after the troublesome lover has departed. "Yeah, he smacked me."

"Last fall Snow smacked you. Does a guy have to hit you before you like him?"

"I didn't say I liked him. I just say this was different. A lot different. I was going to drown." Brace looked into his cup as if he read messages there. "There's more to it than that, but I don't want to talk about it."

"Still," said Howard, "you have to admit that it makes you sound like a pervert."

"I can't help how it sounds." Brace looked up, directly at a portrayal of a bursting gun. He gazed unflinchingly at the blast. "Dane was different coming back on that scow. Told me things. Off the ship he's at least a little different."

Howard supposed to Brace that even crocodiles mellowed.

"That ain't it," said Brace. "I have to find out if I can trust him. I don't want the engine room, but if I can't trust him, I don't want the deck. I'll have to have a transfer." His eyes, for only a moment, shifted from the dusky paintings on the wall. His eyes showed a trace of fear.

"I don't get it."

"These guys owe me something."

"Nothing."

"They do," Brace said. "I have to find out. Do they keep their promises." He butted the cigarette, lit another. "If I went to the engine room, it would leave one man short on deck. I want to know do they keep their promise, even if it shorts the deck."

"So why do you need me?"

"You've been around," said Brace. "I wanta know, is it fair what I'm doing, or am I setting them up?"

"You could be setting your own self up," Howard told him, "but, yes, it's fair."

"I wanted to know," Brace said with smoke-puffing sincerity, " 'cause I'm never going to pull hard for anybody, ever again, ever, unless they don't lie to me."

Howard opined that Brace was going to lead a lonely life.

"If that's the way it's got to be."

"It's a good ship."

"It's a ship," Brace said. "These guys have to be as good with their mouths as they are at sea." He leaned back in the chair, and the intensity that crowded him seemed to concentrate. "Dane rigged that patch. I don't know everything, but I know what I saw."

"You saw a bosun rig a patch," said Howard.

"That's a way of not lying. When you can do that."

"I guess," Howard told him, "that you have to be from Illinois." Howard slurped the last of his coffee, a man eager to make a quick departure.

"Nope," said Brace. "Every time I try to understand this, you, or somebody, wiggles away. Now quit wigglin' and talk."

"What am I supposed to say? We do what we do. It must be worth doing. Otherwise we wouldn't."

"That's what all the liars say." Brace's barely lined face

seemed concentrated on memories of thousands of hundreds of liars. "I don't mean you. That's what my old man used to say about trombones. He could make a trombone sound exactly like a flat tire."

"Every time you guys talk about your fathers, I'm glad I didn't have one."

"But Dane isn't a flat tire. Snow isn't. Or not if they keep their promise . . . " and Brace faltered.

"Okay," said Howard. "We do what we do because dopes can't take care of themselves. The world is mostly dopes and pimps. The pimps can take care of themselves." He rubbed at his empty coffee cup as though it were a crystal ball. He looked into the cup, looked at Brace. "I just lost a friend," he said apologetically. "A dope killed him."

"Only dopes and pimps?"

"I don't know," said Howard. "Scavengers. We're the scavengers, and we pick up the leftovers. We're crows, magpies, basking sharks, gulls. . . . "

"Ohio must be worse than I thought."

"It's not Ohio," said Howard. "It's every place. You asked for this. You enlisted."

"I'm not complaining."

"Yes, you are. But you can't think that Levere and the rest can waste time worrying about what some punk seaman deuce does."

"They better," said Brace, "or else they better start learning to play the trombone."

"If I see an admiral, I'll mention your name." Howard made motion to stand. "I get so sick of drinking. I'm going to a movie."

"One thing."

"Yes."

"You don't believe that about ghosts and Jonahs?"

"I believe it about the ghost," Howard said, and he was grim. "That ghost and I have been around and around—three times."

Howard stood, fished for his money, counted. "I have enough for two, if you have our bus fare back." He looked at Brace, who seemed fascinated by a flaming, crashing mast.

"A Jonah's just another name for bad luck," Howard said. "Maybe it's just another name for weather. We get tore up every year, we break at least one arm every year . . . . " He paused, because his catalog suddenly foundered on a reality. "A guy doesn't get lost every year," he said.

"Is it going to be a funny movie?"

"Comedy," Howard told him. "You call them comedies."

XXI

~~~~~~

ON THE clear winter horizon, a white ship, whitely asparkle with ice.

Downeasters know these days, when the sky raises in the northeast and sunlight flashes, flares, floods, bursts, shatters.

Temperatures drop, drop further, suddenly plunge. The clear air is filled with sparkle. Moisture in the air freezes and pops with sudden brilliant transubstantiation into miniature flakes of ice. The moderate sea foams thickly at the bow. Salt water arcs cream-colored and stiffening toward rails and chains where it freezes, or it falls pebbled into the sea as drops change to pearls of ice in a three- or four-foot travel. The ship becomes a warm cave lined with ice. Brass frames of portholes telegraph the cold. Inside the ship, condensation freezes thick and frosty on the frames. Men sit warm (playing cards, yarning) beneath dull, vanilla halos of ice.

On deck, when a man is unlucky enough to have an errand, breath comes hard through a wool-mufflered nose. The air freezes moisture in the breath. Nose hair is a mat, a clogged and frozen filter through which breath is sucked. Teeth ache from mouthfuls of cold. The thickest and best homemade mittens, of the kind that only Maine women make, seem like thin paper shells. Feet are not stomped. The thickest boots with the thickest liners are only just thick enough. The sparkle and glitter and dance in the air are pinpricks of light; hitting the eyes, making the mind groggy as if the head suffered the aftermath of a blow.

Rigged lifelines are stiff with ice, like coated steel rods. The deck becomes a glaze that would knock the feet from under a cat. Where heaving lines once hung on the rails, there is now empty space. Conally has taken the lines and hung them in Howard's office where they will stay dry. A man cannot heave a frozen coil.

Cutter *Adrian* returned to sea as Lamp's calendar, aplot with menus, flipped to December. Thanksgiving, which Snow thought one of the larger advantages of the New World, lay like a subdued burp in the memory; and Lamp, still in combat with the invisible, confided to Howard, Brace and Conally that Christmas was going to make Thanksgiving look like "pale pink puddin.''

"We been a long time away,'' Conally mourned. "Our ladies will have found other guys.''

Lamp held to the opinion that Conally's "kind of ladies'' had waited no longer than fifteen minutes.

"There's nice girls at the Salvation Army.''

"I don't want to meet somebody who's Salvation Army nice,'' said Brace.

"They have a brass band,'' Howard explained to no one in particular.

On these days of lapse between storms, the coastal waters flourish with traffic. Boats move between ports, shift moorings, make brief dashes toward wintered-in islands. The harbors freeze. Tugs with icebreaker bows plow the narrow road of the channel. Buoy snatchers break off replacement and salvage among wrecked aids to navigation. The snatchers make fast trips to resupply the lighthouses. Men listen to radio Boston, gauge the weather, and the men take thin sniffs at the air, judge the "signs." Sometimes the men take chances.

The ill-prepared and lousy double-ended auto ferry *Islander*, three hundred feet long and taller than a house, en route from Canada to its startling new port of Seattle, ran empty along the coast. It carried a working crew of six men for bringing it through the Panama Canal. In the inshore water, spray mounted the forward end of the low car deck. The thing became like a skating rink—or—the vast, open car deck was like a frozen playing field. As wind arrived, spray ran the length of the car deck. The deck, stanchions, bulkheads became coated. *Islander* resembled a floating tunnel of ice.

Aboard *Adrian*, Brace peeled apples while men sat at tables telling lies about liberties in Boston. Images of eager and easily satisfied women seemed to hover kibitzing above a poker game that, because it was the wrong side of payday, had a nickel limit. In the wardroom, Dane and Levere sat with as much ease as they had ever displayed at sea. They spoke in low tones that Howard, no matter his acute and nosily trained hearing, could not decipher. From forward the engines were as smooth and certain as the low and easy swell beneath *Adrian*'s keel. The ship moved with the rich, studied regularity of a cruise liner peopled by touristing millionaires.

The cracker Bascomb hollered the up cards as he dealt five-card stud. Conally, it seemed, looked at two tens showing. Conally bet two cents, was called. The cards slapped around. Conally dragged a pot worth sixty cents. If Howard had not known Conally well, he would have sworn that Conally was no different than ever.

Lamp appeared in the office doorway and blocked the view of the messdeck. He handed Howard a short list of galley items for the quarterly requisition. Lamp pretended to be all business, and he was not. His red-blond-haired-red-faced head tipped slaunchwise over huge shoulders, and his head seemed like a teacup precariously perched on a cabinet.

"I got something to say," he whispered. "Come forward."

"Where?"

"I think maybe the boat deck," Lamp whispered. "There won't be anybody on the boat deck."

"You gotta be kidding."

"Boat deck," Lamp insisted. He turned and was clearly headed forward to get his gear. Howard stood, plucked his jacket from a hook, kicked off his shoes and began to pull on his boots. He looked up, saw Conally watching. Conally stood, raked in his change. He walked across the messdeck.

"Boat deck," Howard whispered. "Don't asky why."

"I guess I know."

"We don't want a parade."

"There won't be no parade," Conally whispered. "It's gettin' on toward thirty below up there."

In Maine, in December, and with a lot of fat, a lot of thrashing and more luck than comes with loaded dice, a man can live in the water for five minutes. Most men die immediately of shock.

Conally followed Howard. The two men walked across the fiddley, undogged a forward hatch, stepped onto the port side of the main deck. A lifeline angled from a stanchion and forward into the bow. The line was as stiff and hard as cable. Conally reached with a mittened hand, attempted to twang the line. The line creaked. Shatters of ice were like brilliant rain in the sunlight. Thin ice formed on the house, so that the ship momentarily seemed made of mother of pearl. Wind of *Adrian's* passage was light, sharp as an assault by needle points. The men turned their backs to the wind. Conally dogged the hatch.

"This better be about something."

"Nobody said you had to come."

"You an' me," said Conally. "Now we know better."

"Levere knows something he isn't telling," said Howard. "Maybe Dane knows."

"You mean New Bedford?"

"I know how District works. I figure *Abner* to New Bedford, and *Able* comes up here. I figure we ride herd on *Able.*"

"If it ain't no worse than that," said Conally, "then I reckon I could stand it."

"What could be worse?"

Conally looked at the light swell that ran beneath brilliant sunshine. He hunched his shoulders and faced aft.

"Dane's going to take mustang grade," Conally said in a voice of misery. "District is gonna give him *Able.*" Conally conjectured with the certainty of an accused man before a hanging judge. He looked upward at the boat deck, where, leaning against the stack, Lamp stood red-faced and waiting.

"Dane's different," Conally said. "All last month." Conally turned toward the ladder and the boat deck.

Howard followed, shocked with the awful fear that Conally was correct. In his worst imaginings, Howard had never imagined a thing so terrible.

The main deck served as a funnel for ice, and where water splashed and ran toward the scuppers, ice lay in ridges. Close to the house the ice was thin. The two men held rails that were welded to the house. They walked closely and kicked their boots into the angle formed by house and deck.

"You could run hot water pipe," Conally said. "Right under the deck. Like a great big heater."

"Cost a lot. Cost more than this thing's worth."

"I only saying what you could do."

The boat deck was free of ice, but in the scuppers lay small wind pockets of snowy ice wrung from the air. The easy passage of *Adrian* was not fast enough to bring stack fumes to the boat deck. Above the men's heads the warmth flowed like an insulating blanket that mostly obscured the sun and not the cold. Lamp huddled against the stack which was nearly as cold as the surrounding rails and stanchions and deck. Lamp looked at Conally with no surprise or resentment. Lamp looked at Howard. "He's in on it?"

"Isn't everybody?"

"No," said Lamp. "Everybody isn't. Most of the boys have forgot."

"They loaded it off with Masters."

"That's what they did," said Lamp. Lamp leaned against the stack as if he were trying to hold it up. His hooded foul-weather jacket enclosed his face so that he seemed only a red mouth, a red nose existing in a cavern. He had pulled on no foul-weather pants. The thin cotton of his cook's whites stretched across heavy shanks, and his legs were on the road to frostbite. "I've studied it and studied it," said Lamp. "Only I just now got it figured out."

"You sure picked a pretty day."

"I just now figured it out." Lamp looked at Conally, and Lamp's red nose twitched with suspicion. "You ain't going to believe this, boys."

"If I'm not going to believe it," said Howard, "let's go where I can disbelieve it in comfort."

"We had two ghosts," Lamp said earnestly to Conally. "That guy on *Hester C.* was tellin' us about Wilson. Jensen's been telling us about Dane."

Sunlight glanced and flashed from a patch of ice on the fantail. The wake foamed. The cover on the small boat was white with frost that had been distilled from the canvas. A thin line of frost lay on top of the boom that ran above the small boat. The stack purred, colored the clear air with layers of fumes. Conally shifted his weight, looked upward to the flying bridge as if he expected to see spies.

"You're right," said Howard. "I don't believe it."

Conally shifted his weight, hesitated, seemed trying to decide whether to stay or go.

"I kinda do," he said. "Tell me what you figure."

Lamp's figuring, less fulsome than it would have been on a warm messdeck, figured that Jensen would not return. "I told him his job was done. You remember."

"Yes," said Howard.

Lamp's figuring, as intense as any sinner-priest's theology, had followed a predictable course. He "thought 'n thought" and got nowhere. Then, on a day that was not remarkably different from other days, he saw Levere and Dane sitting in the wardroom.

"That's when it hit me. When we saw Jensen, Jensen was sitting in Dane's chair."

"I don't know nothin' about that," said Conally. "Jensen said to look out for ice. Now we got ice."

"We're talking about the best seaman in the world."

"I don't know all the seamen in the world."

"The lines are all rigged," Conally said helplessly. "Hawser's ready to go. Back-up hawser's ready." Conally looked at the ship, turned and looked all around, as if he searched for an enemy.

"Do we have a Jonah? Did we have one?"

"In a manner of speaking," said Lamp. "I've thought an' thought about this."

"Who?"

"I got to get inside," said Lamp. "My legs are freezing." He smacked his thighs, the front of his legs. "A Jonah ain't who, it's what," said Lamp. "A green kid, a yellow snipe . . . . " Lamp faltered before his spectrum of color.

"Sure," said Conally. "I can see that." Conally looked like he had been searching arduously for the right tool and had found it. "There is something a guy can do," he said. "Just keep the kid away from Dane."

Lamp was clearly beginning to suffer from cold, was stiff from leaning against the stack. He stood away from the stack, took a hobbled step, bounced to shake his legs alive. He looked at his feet, and he regretted the bounce. At Lamp's back the stack rumbled, seemed to hesitate, nd then the deepening rumble opened like the low notes of a pipe organ. The men listened, sensed the shaft increasing its whip, saw the stern set slightly lower as *Adrian* put on speed.

"Goin' somewhere," said Conally. "I hope it ain't about anything."

"That's a good kid," Lamp said. "Don't lean."

"Didn't say anything about leanin'," said Conally. "And I got nothing against the punk." He turned to face forward into the needling wind. He looked at the sea. "Twelve knots," he said. "We're full, not flank. Maybe Snow's just blowing coke from the engines." He turned back to Howard and Lamp. "You guys got anything else?" A rain of ice vibrated from the lip of the stack, and the ice was black with diesel exhaust. It shattered, scattered, scampered across the deck like black rain.

"Nothing," said Howard. "Except a chill."

"I still think Dane's gonna take mustang grade," said Conally. "All last month he's been telling me things. Been telling me stuff that's going to need doing next spring."

XXII

DANE DID not die in the tunnel of ice aboard *Islander*, he died because of that tunnel; in a hospital, and he died with dry feet—perhaps the only surprise life ever presented him for which he was not fully prepared.

Ice—be it ever so humble, and as those few know who have raised their eyes beyond the horizons of cocktail glasses—is worth talking about by sailors and poets. While fire at sea is spectacular and fast, ice gives a man time to think. Ice is not whimsical, as fire is sometimes whimsical. Ice is occult, abstract, yet persevering. It requires only the smallest amount of commitment from the sufferer. It is generous in its reward to that commitment.

Dying in company with ice is almost as nice as dying of morphine. A man gets to lie down, give away his busyness, and forget in that permanent haze of fading mortality all of those pranks and sideshows of a world where dealers in death appear as regularly as rows of cabbages at the greengrocer's. Death, dealing a pat hand of ice, seems to understand such calms. If death did not understand, death would not be so certain, so banal.

Cutter *Adrian* punched its screws into the sea and pressed north. On the bridge, Levere and Chappel and Dane planned the best way to accomplish the impossible.

-Three hundred feet—yes, chum, but draft like a ping pong ball—think of the freeboard, that thing's like a sail—have to harness—towing yoke—only way to go—I seen them things, bitts are offset—yoke it then, chief, yoke it. We'll get on radio, try to get a set up—

Howard, summoned to the bridge, stood silent and waited. Dane turned to him, and Dane was imitating Gibraltar. He hunched his shoulders in a clear effort to loosen them, or else in anticipation of finding that handle he needed to pick up and hoist the world. "Fix your watch list. I want Conally, Joyce, Glass and the punk to the bridge. I want them now."

"Technically," said Howard, who engaged in a courageous act, "the kid is still with Lamp."

"Don't give me no technically." Dane's chief's hat was pushed to the back of his head. His forehead seemed to bulge, and it was covered with sweat although the bridge was chilled. His forehead glistened in imitation of an ornamental light bulb. White strands of hair poked from beneath the hat. He flexed his hands. Salt water stains on his foul-weather jacket were white pools on the green fabric, like an abstraction of surf.

"I'm not the world's best seaman." Howard persisted with near desperate courage. "I'm better than Brace."

"Yeah, but you ain't Brace, short timer." Then Dane relented, as though the echo of his own words offended his ears. "The punk has to learn," he said quietly. "I know that you're lots better."

And Howard, fatalistic before a knowledge that he did not understand, and possibly having received a compliment, laid below to carry his errand.

Ice hung in dull circles as condensation froze on the ports.

The brass dogs on hatches were covered with frost, brittle looking, like calcimine. As Howard crossed the fiddley, the hot air rising through the grates warmed his legs, but his shoulders felt the chill that radiated through the hull. Chief engineman Snow ascended the ladder from the engine room.

"These double-enders have two drive lines," said Snow. "What is the problem, exactly?"

"I'm no engineman. I think the thing only has one transmission."

Islander, certified in all respects ready for sea, had suffered a burned clutch. It was drifting toward the sharp waters near Bibb Rock, and it was an odds-on chance that the ferry was going to fetch the rock. The inshore wind was at twenty knots. *Islander*, streamed to a jury-rigged sea anchor, was drifting at half a knot.

"I must speak with their engineman." Snow flitted from the fiddley, toward the bridge.

On the steaming messdeck, men waited for news. Brace sat and stared at the accomplished fact of a vat of peeled apples. *Adrian* rose and fell with slight and distant shocks as the increased speed pressed it against the easy sea.

"Come to the office," Howard told Conally, and Howard's voice was small and strained with his fear.

Conally stepped into the office. His swarthy Indian face, which was usually a mask of reserve, wrinkled with omen. He attempted to readjust his face, resume his mask. Failed.

"You're supposed to take Glass and Joyce to the bridge," said Howard. "You're supposed to take the kid, too."

"What's goin' on? What?"

"I don't know what's going on. Don't know."

"Do you think Lamp's right?"

"Yeah," said Howard. "Lamp's right. So is Dane." He paused, and he was as helpless as Conally. "Maybe the crazy part isn't over," he said. "Maybe Dane is nuts."

"There's six guys on that thing."

"I don't know what that means. We'll do our best. What does that mean?"

"I dunno," said Conally. "Maybe I'm nuts, too." He turned to leave, turned back like a clipped apology. "I'll do what I can," he said. "I'll try to stay between them." He stepped to the messdeck and began hollering, swearing. Glass and Joyce stood, grabbed their gear, ran. Brace picked up the vat of apples, carried them to the galley, moving with approximately the grace and speed of a cow en route to a barbecue. Howard, rushing, brushed past—stopped.

"Get moving."

"I'm moving," Brace told him. "Just as fast as I promised to move, when people lie to me." Brace refused to look at Howard, but Brace's face was shamed, and it was clear that Brace was lying. He sat the vat of apples on the deck of the galley, looked up, and saw the awesome figure of Lamp standing above him and looking down.

"You're lying, sonny. Get truthful and get moving."

"It's an emergency," Howard said. "It has nothing to do with what we talked about. It has nothing to do with whether you go to engine room or deck."

"It does have to do with what we talked about, but not the engine room. It's worse than that." Brace's eyes showed a hint of unreasonable fear.

"Get moving, sonny." Lamp bent, picked up an apple, tossed it, caught it. "We mostly serve these in a pig's mouth. After we roast him."

Brace moved.

"Yellow?" Howard stood in momentary disbelief.

"Naw," said Lamp. "He ain't yellow, but he sure is trembly, ain't he?"

The small bridge, when Howard returned, seemed packed with *Adrian*'s entire crew. The increased speed caused spray to rise at the bow. In the sunshine, the light spray became pale feathers of blown ice; like a sown blessing from an apostolic hand creating parables of seed on rocky ground. The ice fell to the decks in hoar flakes and pebbles.

"I want crash mats on the bow," Levere told Dane. "Rig them while we still have daylight."

"Phil—cap—" Dane faltered as he displayed a familiarity with Levere that the crew had never before heard. "The plates won't take it."

"Will the line?"

Dane slumped, and he momentarily looked like a stubbed cigar butt. Then he straightened, stomped a foot. "If we don't get more wind. If we can get it head to wind, let the wind blow through it instead of agin it." He stomped his foot again, either to shock his rheumatism into obedience, or in a display of anger.

Howard, who in later years would have more than several occasions to wonder if he had ever done anything correctly, would—in those later years—recall one thing.

"I want to be in on this," he told Dane. "I don't care what you think."

"You'll be on the helm," said Chappel.

"Use Rodgers."

"You are the best helm after Glass."

"Glass is going to be on deck," said Glass, "and if you don't like it, you can book Glass, later."

"You will be on the helm," Chappel told Howard.

Men stood, sweated with compacted closeness, with tension. They jammed together on the bridge—Conally, Dane, Snow, Joyce, Chappel, Brace, Glass, Levere, Howard—shuffled, sweated. Quartermaster designate Rodgers over-corrected on the helm, spun it back, was silent and attentive to the compass as he chewed on Chappel's estimate of helmsmen. Rodgers began to speak, thought better of it, remained silent. Brace looked toward Howard, and Brace had his back to Dane.

"I suppose," Brace whispered in a voice of absolute despair, "if you've seen one engine room you've seen 'em." The trace of fear was still in his eyes.

Snow, standing across the bridge and with the radio transmitter in one hand, was turned sideways to Brace. He did not see Brace's eyes, but he heard Brace's words. He turned to Brace. Snow's eyes showed contempt, but his voice was level and implied nothing to any other man on the bridge. "Have you something to say?"

Brace flushed, pawed helplessly at the pocket of his dungaree shirt as if he searched for his heart. The flush rose from his neck, made his ears glow as certainly as neon. The flush ran across his cheeks and forehead. He began to speak, stuttered, became silent.

Dane looked at Levere, and Levere was looking forward into the rapidly icing bow. Light spray rose, sparkled, dimmed into white flakes of ice. Sunlight bleached the bow, and the hooded three-inch-fifty gun looked like a schoolteacherly white finger, admonishing the sea.

"There ain't nothing else we can do." Dane turned to Conally. "You think of anything, Jim?" He turned to Snow. "Ed?"

"I think," said Snow, "that we are capable of repairing the clutch. If you can keep it from the beach for two hours, I believe I may promise power on one drive line."

"They haven't got any hawser," said Levere. "You'll have to rig the yoke."

If Dane had ever been disconcerted, no man could recall having seen the event. Dane stood, squat, compact as a stump, and like a stump, at least temporarily immobile. Then he shifted his weight, flipped at the underside of his nose with the back of his hand—for the enjoyment. He looked at Brace, and Brace was ablush and silent. Dane's voice was thick with scorn. "I was on an icebreaker, once. Convoy to Murmansk."

Dane turned toward Conally. Glass stepped back to tread heavy on Howard's feet. Dane began to bulge, swell, prepare his blast. Joyce faltered. Joyce stepped backward, trod heavily on Howard's feet.

"You are a bunch of punks," Dane said kindly. "You are ladies at a garden party . . . and now, ladies, if you have finished sippin' at your tea . . . " The blast arrived:

Tuck up your skirts—ladies—tuck 'em up and get crackin'.

Dane wheeled, like a man trying to take first advantage in some dark contest. He was first off the bridge, first onto the main deck, and he moved aft as certainly as an army tank. He did not bother to slam his feet into the angle formed by house and deck.

"Stand by for a moment," Snow said to Brace, as Conally, Joyce and Glass fled as if pulled by strings. Snow's small face, in the light shadow of the sunlit bridge, was not elfish. It looked not exactly old, yet it was creased, weathered, strangely and suddenly thin-lipped. "I do not break promises," said Snow, "and I do not value your silly accusations."

Brace seemed ready to faint. He no longer blushed. His face was pale.

"Your apology will not be accepted this time," Snow told him. "Acceptance must be earned. As Chief Dane has just remarked, I suggest that you get cracking."

Snow turned back to the radio, preparatory to seeking more information from *Islander*. Brace stood, puffed, panted, zipped at his foul-weather jacket. He staggered from the bridge, and he rocked from blows that were clearly delivered by the heavy hammers of shame.

Levere turned to Howard. "Stand by." He walked to the hatch, undogged it, and he stood on the wing looking aft. Ice swelled and built in the bow, and the spray was extending the ice further along the decks. The fantail was slick with a thin layer of it, but the fantail was not deadly, as the bow was deadly. Levere watched the action as men began laying out hawser to form a yoke. Levere's face, slightly swollen, dark, hawklike, French, Yankee; seemed for a moment ready to mutate into a mask of tears. Then he muttered something incomprehensible. From the bow, spray rose. Light feathers of ice hit Levere's jacket and lodged in his hair. He turned to enter the bridge.

"The eighty-three boat from Kennebunkport is underway," he told Howard. "It won't arrive in time, but it may arrive in time to do something."

"If we only had *Abner*—"

"We don't," Levere said. "We have towing line and alternatives. I want to give you instructions." Levere paused, watching Howard critically, wondering, no doubt, if he had the right man for the job.

"Sometimes," said Levere, "if you can't pull, you can still push. Now, that is not a tugboat helm. It will seem to react a good deal more quickly. The hull will skid."

Howard, suppressing thoughts of those whispering bow plates, creaking, strung weak with age, listened to instructions on how to steer a tugboat.

XXIII

〰〰〰〰〰〰〰〰〰〰〰〰〰〰〰〰〰〰〰〰〰〰〰〰〰〰〰〰〰〰〰〰〰

TWO VESSELS dancing. A slow dance between ill-matched partners; *Islander*, thick, fat, hollow. *Adrian* a wisp, a sliver, like a small, objecting white blade prancing before the loud mouth of the land; before the white line of frozen water marking the high point where white surf ran, rumbled, threw ice and ice-coated debris toward the land. *Adrian* circled the iceberg hulk of *Islander*, which in the darkness of early evening was aglow with light. The car deck glistened, a sheet of ice, across which ran thinly etched lines, the shadows of lifelines.

Islander pivoted broadside to the surf at *Adrian's* approach. Figures of men on the car deck hauled the thin line of the sea anchor, and from the crossing stern of *Adrian* the etching of a heaving line curved flatly into the wind. It hit a man in his raised hands, and he looked like an outfielder shagging a fly.

"I did it," Brace yelled. "Me."

"Get it down next time, you cow milker. Get it lower."

Yeoman Howard, running like a skein of snoopiness through

memory, conversation, and through the log, would someday "get the picture."

Both vessels straightened. They angled directly seaward as hawser came taut on short tow; the hawser with its tons shaking flakes of ice as *Adrian* sat its stern into the sea. The stern rose slowly, the ship clawed toward the sea. The engines churned at three-quarters, then rose nearly to full.

"If we can get a little sea room."

"We're getting some."

"Where's that rock?"

"Ain't your business, chummy. Let the cap worry."

"I reckon it's my business."

On the glazed fantail, beneath floodlights that turned the iced decks into wan sheets of treachery, men stood, retreated backward; waited to lengthen the tow. Men crouched behind iced gear lockers, and wind pebbled the lockers with an increasing assault of ice as inshore water smacked the hull, rose, was blown across the fantail.

"I hate this part. I hate this worst of all."

"Maybe it'll hold."

"Stand back, there, clowns, stand back. The line is goin' thin."

Adrian dashed forward, hesitated, ran quickly seaward as the hawser parted; one length rising in a whipping, arcing, snake-like, boldly-moving line above the fantail. The other length fell atrail of *Islander* and sagged toward the surf where it indifferently streamed like a web waiting to foul the propellers of anybody's ship.

"You hurt, chum?"

"It's moving. I can move it. I don't think it's broke." Gunner Majors rose, fell back toward the scupper, rose slowly. He grabbed a chain, fell forward, twisting, like a man tackled.

"Help him below."

"Get Lamp."

"Get hauling on that line, get haulin'."

"My gut hurts. That's mostly what it is."

"Get him below."

"I do it," said Majors. "I do it by myself." He once more hauled himself erect. He stood trembling. He bent sideways, on a slaunch, panting as he accommodated a couple of broken ribs. He moved slow and crablike from the deck, and he braced himself against stanchions and chains.

The short line came in, hauled by hands that came away sticky from the hawser as ice rapidly formed and seemed attempting to steal mittens. The line was short and did not need to be walked. Across the fantail men skidded, to ride, to slide to their knees as they attempted to set up a new rig. *Adrian* crashed forward in the building inshore water. Blown ice, no larger than mist, was like a thin cloud about the ship. Dane stood above the men, watched them scrabble and claw, watched *Islander.*

"Belay that. They're dropping line."

Aboard *Islander,* men hung desperately to lifelines, tied themselves to lifelines, and attempted to recover the broken hawser.

"Not a chance. They don't have a winch. Offshore without a winch."

"They got nothing," said Dane, and he was disgusted. "No winch, no hawser, no spare parts. Nothin'."

Aboard *Islander* one side of the yoke was freed, then, moments later, the other side. The towline slid toward the surf like a dying snake.

"It's all they could do. I reckon it is."

"Where's that rock?"

"If we double up on one bitt . . . "

"Can't tow that way, can't tow on a slaunch."

"Dear Jesus, Jesus dear, it's cold."

On those northern shores, when the wind sets north-northeast above that line where land and water meet, the surf holds claws, steeples of rock, the discarded tops of mountains—and to be spit onto those shores through that rocky surf is a certain warrant that a man has misplaced his faith in something—towline, perhaps.

Yeoman Howard climbed across the small helm like a tortured prisoner on a wheel, as *Adrian* came about, while *Islander* again swung broadside the surf. Close to land, the swells began to build. The water seemed to move closer together in a gesture of frozen companionship. *Adrian* rose, fell, jolted, jolted again. As Levere brought his vessel into the lee of *Islander*, *Adrian* rattled like an empty freight car on rough track. A white sheet of ice fell from the flying bridge, dropped before Howard's eyes; a slate on which might be written the names of men. Defrosters on the bridge chuffed, whirled, blew. The glass panes between helmsman and sea were streaked, running with icy glaze through which the icy bow appeared. The caked ice in the bow blanked the dead eyes. The anchor chain was buried beneath ice. Ice rose from the mats of woven hawser that hung over the bow, the ice rising above the mats like small walls of ice.

"I have the eighty-three boat on the horn," said Chappel. "I'm sure it is the contact."

"Distance."

"An hour."

"Lay us alongside," said Levere. "Our engineers have no luck." He paused. "I hope they have some."

Chappel droned, was calculating as he droned. "Bibb Rock bears two-two-zero, range eighteen hundred." Levere did easy sums, as did Howard and radioman James.

"Chief Dane to the bridge. The faster we get alongside . . ."

"Cap, if we can clear that rock, we'll have the time."

"We'll clear."

Radioman James laid aft like a wisp, a quick moving spirit, to fetch Dane. *Adrian* lay rolling in *Islander*'s lee. *Islander*'s crew grasped lifelines, passed lines, leaned forward to grasp the hands of Snow and McClean. A canvas tied to bursting with asbestos and shims and springs was drawn aboard with a line.

Dane appeared on the bridge, followed by James, and Dane stomped up the ladder in spite of feet that were surely almost frozen. His foul-weather jacket was wet with melting ice. His mouth was clamped tight, thin, froglike, in control; and Dane was cold and clearly on the raw edge of control. He huffed as he stomped. The fathometer went click-whickety-whickety.

"We'll tow from the starboard cleat," Levere told Dane. "Try to get sea room. At least we can swing it sharp down wind."

"Short tow. Double the line."

"Take some men." Levere looked forward, into the bow which carried a burden of ice that canted *Adrian* heavily forward into the sea. The bow shook, shed ice, added more. The buildup on deck was so great that it was impossible to tell where the deck ended and the rails began. A faint sound flashed from aft as ice in hundred-pound hunks crashed to the boat deck.

"If I have to shove the thing," Levere said, "I'll take it on the starboard quarter, turn it end for end to spin it."

"You want fenders. Crash mats. They don't have 'em."

Levere looked at Dane, and in the red lights of the bridge Levere's face was shadowed, stern. "All they have is you," he said. "As a matter of fact, all *we* have is you."

"That Conally," said Dane. "Now he's a good kid, and he has the deck. That punk Joyce, now he just ain't so bad." Dane wiped the back of his hand across his thin mouth, then flipped water from his hand. "Phil . . . bust this thing one more time, and they'll hang you."

"With a short drop," Levere told him. "Ops is already telling me that I'm a shipkiller."

"This iron's been dead for twenty years."

"You know it," said Levere, "and I know it."

"Key to the arms locker," said Dane by way of a request. "I got a notion, and gunner Majors caught hisself a little trouble."

"Now that should be logged," said Chappel. "What is the nature of the trouble?" He turned, horse headed from the radar.

"He got some clothesline across his gut," said Dane. "What's the range, quartermaster?"

Chappel, wordless, stepped back to the radar. Levere fished for his keys.

"Lamp is tapin' him," said Dane. "Don't worry."

"I wish I didn't hear all this." James spoke, but he did not take his eyes, his face, his stance, his effort from the fathometer. "Seven-eight," he said, "and take me with you, chief. We got water 'til near all the way in."

Dane stomped, opened his frog mouth, looked at the puniest, weak-

est man aboard. He began to say no. He stared at the deck like a philosopher immersed in a grand platitude. "Get your clump aft the minute you get relief. I'll send Rodgers to relieve." To Levere, Dane said, "A guy could take the helm and still give engine orders." He spun from the bridge, stomping down the ladder like a troll that walks where and when it wills.

"Stay on the helm," said Levere. "Chief Dane has a lot on his mind."

Howard, who in later years would have cause to wonder if he had ever done anything correctly, thankfully stayed on the helm.

Opening the arms locker with Levere's keys, Dane ignored the line-throwing gun which was the only weapon that *Adrian* had ever earnestly used. He climbed aboard *Islander*, and he was packing a .45 pistol. Dane looked like a top sergeant leading an attack uphill. Behind him Glass, Brace and James followed like hooded monks in attendance on one crusade or another. The men rigged a doubled line to the starboard cleat of

Islander, then disappeared from the iced deck as *Adrian* once more turned into the sea.

When the line parted the second time, men fell along icy decks, attempted to recover line, and they banged against stanchions, sprawled like squashed spiders. They braced their feet against the stanchions, against piles of backup hawser, against lockers. They lay on their backs, braced, rose to grab line, fell backward as it came aboard. The line shook drops of water that laid a funnel of ice along the deck over which the line ran. The line was like a frayed end of failure, and the men heaped it on deck with contempt, with fear, with hatred.

Above the crash of surf, and distant on the car deck of *Islander*, Dane's pistol popped like a small and unimportant theory, as Dane—knowing that he did not have time for sophisticated equipment like marlinspikes—blew holes through every mattress he could find in *Islander*'s cabins. Brace and James, with Glass as a desperate and cooperating overseer, ran line through the holes and tied the mattresses into bulky lumps, overlays of padding that would have to serve for crash mats. The mats looked like overstuffed, cartoon pillows as *Adrian*, with the port searchlight flaring, closed slowly onto *Islander*'s starboard quarter. In the sharp, glaring light, Dane's face seemed two dimensional, white and blanched and worried; as only a face can look when it views what it considers will be disaster. Glass, Brace and James stood beside Dane, attending the lines, ready to adjust the crash mats.

Somehow, and Howard would never know if Levere had made the correct command decision, nor would Levere, the plates held. *Adrian* dug in with its screws. Ice cracked from the bow in shatters, chunks, massive sheets. The great bulk of *Islander* moved in a slow spin to seaward, shoved turning in a pirouette of slow motion so that it slid past the rock with something under a hundred yards to spare. Conally rigged towline. The 83 boat arrived. What one vessel could not do, two vessels could. *Islander* was pulled seaward as Snow and

McClean repaired the clutch. *Islander* proceeded to Boston under its own power.

In the last minutes, as lights flared and every man on both vessels held his breath, perhaps prayed, and certainly talked to steel plates, the best seaman in the world lost his title.

Dane backed from the scene, away from the flashing ice that still splintered from *Adrian*'s bow which hovered like a crazily dressed spectre above *Islander*'s open-ended deck. Dane turned toward the inner recess of the car deck, headed for the bridge and the radio. He walked aft as a sheet of ice rattled loose from *Islander*'s superstructure.

The ice crashed about Dane. In the brilliant light the ice turned into an explosion of sparkles, cold fire, prisms; and Dane momentarily stood in the explosion like a figure of myth consumed by flames. Then he fell, slid, flailed across the open end of the car deck, and he grasped for lifelines and did not find them; a squat form with short, waving arms, and he was followed by Brace, who, like a football lineman faked into a wrong move, recovers only in time to get one hand on a runner's arm. Brace skidded beside Dane, struggling, missing the life lines too; then Brace had a streak of beginner's luck. He skidded hard into a steel pole on the lip of the deck—the pole designed to hold a guard line to restrain future commuters from simplemindedness, from premature advances on their busy and important rounds. Brace hit the pole with one arm, and that arm went limp. He spun, hooked his knees on the pole like an acrobat on a swing, and he kept his grip on Dane's arm. Dane spun forward, over the lip of the low deck, and into the sea. For moments in the flaring lights all that could be seen was Dane's hand rising above the deck and held in Brace's failing grasp, as white water framed the background, as white water rose and thickly turned to ice.

Glass moved, skidded, and James flipped a heaving line after Glass, the line arriving like a throw to home. Glass caught the line, skidded to a stop, grabbed the pole in one hand—grabbed Dane's arm with the other. Glass stepped on Brace, kicked Brace's face in his scramble, and Dane struggled back aboard.

From topside in the superstructure another piece of ice crashed down, and it seemed to fill the night with sparkle. Brace tried to stand, gazed stupidly at his dangling arm, and then he settled in a curled slump around that pole as surely as Amon had ever curled beneath a table.

XXIV

~~~~~~

PNEUMONIA, WHICH is not humble, and which cynics call the enemy of youth and the friend of the aged, attended *Adrian* as the ship beat north at flank speed, homeward bound. Pneumonia, unlike fire and ice, is not worth talking about by sailors and poets. While fire is spectacular, and ice is occult, pneumonia is a cheap theatrical trick that waits in the wings. When a man is exhausted, cold, or injured, pneumonia steps toward the final chorus. Young men often manage to drive it away, old men almost never do.

Adrian jolted and fled across the winter sea, as Snow and Howard traveled like foolish birds of passage between the dying man who lay in the chief's quarters, and the two men who were making their own fights in the crew's compartment. Majors was gussied up and fanciful with codeine, murmuring of miraculous guns. Brace had his own taste of pneumonia. Since neither Howard nor Snow knew if sedation would drop Brace's defense against disease, they sedated him very little; and Brace, on the thrusting, rocking, jolting bunk, no doubt suffered.

Howard spoke to him, but Brace was mostly mute. He confided to Howard that he was "figuring something out."

Lamp held together the after part of the ship by talk and food—Lamp rendering a state of grace on the messdeck to match the same business which Levere attended to on the bridge.

The Indian Conally, in spite of the weather, stalked the boat deck in the wind, a man engaged in an act of communion, perhaps; perhaps in a sacrifice, or a demonstration of faith. Perhaps Conally was only confused.

Glass and James were not talking, not even to each other; and they sat on the messdeck in a sort of stunned silence, as they slurped coffee, and stared into the depths of their mugs like men freshly reacquainted with concepts of infinity. Even the loudmouth cracker Bascomb walked hushed.

Howard, as helpless as a revivalist facing reality, and with dull wits, watched the ancient and vibrating decks. Howard did not understand what he saw, and while Lamp bustled, and—may any stray forces of light, if they are worthy, protect and preserve the soul of Reeser Lamp—actually made chicken soup which Dane refused and so did Glass, Howard turned to Snow; for Howard had catalogued more facts than he could handle.

Snow stood beside Dane. Dane lay drawn, old. His thin hair was white across his pink and dying skull. He breathed in gulps and chokes. His thin lips pulled tight, like a circle of wire around his gulping mouth. He muttered to a woman, called a woman, unnamed here and forever unnamed. Sometimes he cursed. Sometimes he gave orders.

"Why do we put up with this," asked Howard, and he spoke as if he was the youngest man alive. "You've been around, chief. Why do *you* put up with this?"

"I am a seaman," said Snow. "Do you truly want to know?" Snow stood beside Dane's bunk. Snow braced himself against the sharp pitch of *Adrian* as the ship crashed forward on strained engines; and it was clear that Snow then neither thought nor cared about engines. His small face was creased. His mouth was tight when Dane rambled coherently. Snow's mouth relaxed only a little when Dane was incoherent.

"I want to know," Howard said. "All of this means something. I used to be able to figure anything out. I used to know everything."

"As did I," said Snow. "A Scots lad gave me my instruction. He struck me in the mouth at a time when our destroyer was machine-gunning survivors from a submarine. They were swimming toward us. I recall that I was laughing." Snow leaned against a bulkhead, a small brown bird at rest, peering either at half a minute or half a century. "In the war," he said, "we were glad to indulge in madness. When the war was finished, we were still glad to indulge in madness. The reason I put up with this is that it is not madness."

Howard, discovering that he might not yet be a seaman, was awed. "It's embarrassing, what I'm going to do."

"Do you believe," said Snow, and he spoke with absolute wonderment, "you Yanks are a curious people, and with strangely vivid explanations. I am about to use one. Do you actually believe that there is a free lunch?"

Lamp, the magic man, the spiritualist, who immediately understood—after the fact—why Jensen wanted Brace on deck and not in the engine room, behaved like a creative demon of food. He worked through the night, through the morning, and when *Adrian* put lines on the pier and Dane and Brace and Majors were taken ashore, Lamp sagged against a chain, and he was exhausted. He looked over the familiar home harbor of Portland where the channel was a black and narrow river running between ledges of ice. He looked to the mudflats, attempting to discover the ugly form of *Hester C.*; saw only the wreckage of a beat-up work boat scattered by storm along the tide line. Belowdecks, in warm spaces, men shook themselves like dogs ruffling out wet fur. They belched, burped, like old

Romans waiting to get on with the feast. They returned to the messdeck where food lay steaming in glorious redundancy. The men muttered, were not hopeful, but began to feel that they might soon feel that way.

Yeoman Howard, headed to the Base where he would not pick up mail for yeoman Wilson, or for *Abner,* but only mail for *Adrian,* picked up an unusual creature instead. The creature's name was Iris.

"A real winner," the OD at the Base told Howard. "I'm glad you've got the punk."

Steward apprentice Iris, it developed, was a man who had been so gorgeously conned that no argument, no set of reasons, could convince him that the entire world was not in a state of error. During the short walk between Base and ship, Iris managed to explain three times that a recruiter in Hawaii had promised him a change in rate the minute he hit the States. Iris managed to explain four times that he had an engineering degree from a great and powerful university, and that the recruiter had promised that a man with such qualifications would immediately be sent to officer's candidate school. Steward apprentice Iris—who did not have a Chinaman's chance in a Turkish harem of getting a change in rate (being Hawaiian), leave alone O.C.S., and who doubtless had his sheepskin with him—was tall and spectacled and mildly oriental, if one discounted the indignant and confused expression on his face. Yeoman Howard, who was busy mistrusting all experience, kept his big mouth shut. He took Iris aboard and introduced him to bosun striker Joyce.

"What'd I do with him?"

"Square him away," said Howard. "I'll log it. See you below in a minute."

The minute stretched to five, because of the pickiness of the horse-headed Chappel. Chappel hunched above Iris's service record which lay glistening in stiff, new, undented covers. Chappel tsked and pursed his mouth and made worry noises.

Chappel did not have an engineering degree. *Adrian* did not have a chief bosun. All that Howard had was a thick envelope from Personnel which he feared to open.

The logging-in ceremony completed to Chappel's scrupulous satisfaction, Howard laid below; where, with engineering certitude, steward apprentice Iris was hogging the whole show. He had gathered quite a crowd.

"You are a punk," Joyce was telling Iris. "We don't need your flak."

"You must not speak to me in that manner. I have an engineering degree."

"You are a punk with an engineering degree."

"This is the cutter *Adrian*," said Glass. "The captain is Phil Levere, mustang. The man on deck is Jim Conally. The cook is Reeser Lamp. You are steward apprentice Iris."

"You dislike me because I am Hawaiian."

"True," said Wysczknowski, "but yids are worse. And admirals."

"You slant-eyes is all alike," Joyce advised Iris. "We'd ought to pack up the lot of you and send you back to Philadelphia."

"And Polacks," Glass told him. "There ain't nothin' worse than a Polack. I had a long weekend with a Polack lady once . . . by mistake . . . you can take my word."

"Niggers," said McClean. " . . . now I know something about this."

"What are you saying? What in the world are you trying to say?"

"We are saying," said Wysczknowski with considerable ease, "that there is an old, tired guy back aft, and he has been up all night and cooking. So unpack that sloppity seabag . . . . "

"And get crackin'."

The fat envelope, when Howard opened it, contained orders:

The dying Dane was ordered to take command, not of *Able*, but *Aaron* in Boston. Levere had *Able*. The captain of *Aaron* was to take *Adrian*, a grand swapping around that Howard did not then recognize as a rejuvenating and reaffirming principle. All Howard knew was that the auxiliary orders allowed Levere to take some men with him to subdue the jinx ship. Levere had been scrupulous in his requisitions. He had not wanted to short *Adrian.*

Fallon stayed, but Snow was transferred with Levere. Chappel went with Levere, as did Joyce and Wysczknowski, Glass and James. Howard, not knowing whether it was a compliment, a disgrace, or neither, was not included.

XXV

WE OLD men, those of us who are not sand-
papered flat, as we pontificate from the depths of comfortable
chairs, are apt to lie, pretending that chance, youth, dreams and
fortitude are bold matters of understood intent. The truth is
elsewhere. We fumbled, we puzzled, and if we found any great
meanings, the discoveries, like as not, were by plain luck.

Adrian returned to piling seas. As engineman Fallon had
done the winter before, taking over from the senior Jensen, now
the Indian Conally walked the decks for Dane. Conally resembled a blunt hammer as he pounded a new deck gang into
shape.

District offices, frustrated in the appointment of Dane, re-
tained *Aaron's* captain aboard *Aaron*. District sent *Aaron's*
chief bosun, freshly transformed to mustang, to *Adrian*. The
new captain was Ed Chaney. He was an easygoing spendthrift
ashore, a tough and unsleeping sailor the moment that the ship
found deep water. He did not suit Conally, exactly; and he did
not suit Howard, exactly; but each man had to admit that in any

world of fools, Chaney was not going to qualify for merit badges.

Through piling seas *Adrian* towed *Mirabelle, Eben, Lorna Ann, Catspaw, Vicky R.* and *Knight Ethelred* . . . a manly yacht.

From south came news that the decommissioned cutter *Ajax*, rusting on the scrap pile in Boston, was sold to a man who planned to turn it into a small and intimate seaside resturant.

Cutter *Adrian* fought a fire at the coal yards in Portland. Ice once more formed in the bow, and ice sprinkled as drops fell from the high arcs of water, while men skidded across the decks and fought to stay afoot and in command of the heaving, pulsing hoses. The fire was red and gold against the backdrop of the whitened city, and black smoke rose to distribute the miserable smell of sulphur through the ship.

Seaman apprentice Brace refused sick leave, having nowhere to go, and he hung around the Base as an ambulatory patient—but he resembled, in his anxiety to "get on with it," a blind pup in a sausage factory. Conally spoke to Chaney, and Chaney read Levere's comments in Brace's service record. Brace became a full seaman, albeit a seaman with a temporarily unuseable arm.

Cutter *Adrian* towed *Daniel, Misty*, and, on a day of glory, met cutter *Abner* at sea as *Abner* was returning home. *Adrian* and *Abner* closed, men waved, and then the two ships kicked apart on diverging courses to search for the overdue *Dominick* which was found two days later by dune pounders as the disabled vessel swung at the pick in shoal water.

Adrian towed *Violet, Pride Of The Banks, Obadiah.*

Abner, in an excess of family feeling, towed *Sister Sue, Seven Sisters, The Brothers.*

Able towed *Erasmus.*

Word from south spread through the fleet, and the word said that cutter *Able* was "takin' a turn" and "lookin' good." *Able* towed *Jacqueline, Prester John II, Rockrose. Able* searched and found the overdue and written-off *Maiden Of Mist*, adrift with a starving crew that had been reduced to its next to last bottle of booze.

A thirty-six foot lifeboat was declared excess by the Base. It was invoiced as a gift to a troop of sea scouts. From north came radio gossip which hoped for the early breakup of the ice.

Adrian towed *Whisper, Fife, Excalibur.*

Brace, healed and moving silently, slipped into the valued position that had once been held by Glass. Conally confided to Howard that Brace was "gettin' to be dependable." Brace, as mum as the library from which he withdrew books, spent his off-watch time on the messdeck. He read thrillers, mostly fiction, but thrillers, certainly.

Adrian towed *Adrienne,* a possibly incestuous project, which, as Lamp gloomily observed, "just sooner or later *had* to happen." During the time of that tow, the State of Maine turned toward the glorious state of spring.

In Maine in spring, the interminable days of March disappear with a kind of final vengeance, a well-delivered backhand of wind and sleet and rain. April offers a cold cacophony of rain. Rain runs in the brick streets, and it pounds into the plowed facades and banks and pillars and stockades of snow. The piled snow is like a fort besieged, gradually giving way and breaking down before the blows of an inexorable invader. Crud and dirt, grime, soot from wood fires, bleeds darkly from roofs, washes into the streets, and disappears toward the harbor. Old men stretch, yawn, interrupt their yarning to look through wet windows at the dismal weather. The old men read the "sign." Young men hunger and begin to laugh, and the young men are unamazed by tales.

Yeoman Howard, who had looked forward to blowing his reenlistment bonus on bountiful women and a dandy hotel room, found instead that he was groping. He was still young, but he did not feel at all young anymore. With a desperation that he could not then understand, he threw himself at work, gave over to work, and thus, soon ran out of work. The days rolled past, boring, incomplete. Howard, for the first time ever, thought of the future. He decided to change his rate, take a one-grade bust and reenlist as a junior quartermaster. As spring arrived in green splashes, and as liberty was granted, Howard went ashore. Drinking.

The beer tasted just elegant, but it no longer held the alcoholic bite of perfectly inferred freedom. In the bars the jukeboxes blared, and the women seemed to laugh louder and longer at dull jokes. Dane's shack job, Flossie, sat every night at a table beside a chief damage controlman. The silken, stitched tiger on the rolled sleeve of Howard's tailormades was slightly frayed.

The women laughed, haw, haw.

Howard typed his reenlistment papers, signed them, tucked them in his desk. He went ashore, got drunk, really drunk falling-on-his-face-in-it drunk. Conally dragged him back to the ship. Howard slept, woke, showered, muzzled coffee beneath the protective and concerned eyes of Lamp. In two days, when Howard was sure he was sober, truly certain, he opened the desk drawer and tore up the reenlistment.

YMCAs, where young lads run naked and screaming through the hallways as they snap each other on the butts with wet towels, are the curse of the forlorn, the lost, the wanderer; and any YMCA can eventually cure most men of inambition. Howard nosily visited YMCAs, a grand tour of Y's in Boston, New York, Winston-Salem. He toured the coast, saw cutter *Abner* on one occasion, cutter *Able* on another. He visited Fairhaven, Newport News. He decided that he must leave the coast. He thought that if he left the coast he might feel young again; return to youth.

He toured the heartland, was revolted. The cow colleges, the house trailers, the daft certainty. Like a man intent on suicide, he pressed on to California. He drank, but he did not get so drunk that he could not find the bus station in L.A. He fled back east, wandered along the docks. He fished for a season, thought of going for a purser's ticket in the merchant marine; dismissed the thought.

He seemed nudged by a hand that momentarily extended from the invisible world, touching his shoulder, returning him to Boston.

It was in Boston, he told himself, that he would have to "make or break," and, although he did not understand why, he still did understand that awful proposition that is not a myth, but true. Because it was in Boston—no matter how bloody and wrongheaded and fire filled the history might be—it was in Boston that the primer had been written. It was in Boston that he gained a sense, a first and original taste of a new kind of youth. He discovered that, after all, he was not a man who made history, but a man who studied history. In an excess of redeemed youth, and of beautiful and certain ignorance, he began his work.

He worked well during his thirties, mastering the facts, sweeping instinctively with the flow, feeling intuitively that the slowly rolling wheel of events would someday, and soon, make mists of confusion flow away as before a night wind. He got married, the first time to a singer, the second time to a librarian; but, in spite of his attentions, the women became bored, somehow. They found other and more clever companionship.

In his early forties, he found himself pondering matters over which other heads—and better, doubtless—had already pondered. He added to the matters a small touch here, an addition there. His accomplishments, if they were accomplishments, produced works that better heads in the future might ponder, use, if only to disprove. He again married, a fellow historian, and that woman chose to stay beside him.

In his late forties he enjoyed a flurry of hope, good will, and he worked well. He believed, with some justice, that he had an original notion. He thought, studied, worked, turned fifty.

Through the pages of the past, and all about him in the present, messiahs spoke with thrilling commands. Politicians and generals spoke in warm, even-heated, thrilling commands—of national honor and pride as they dealt in disgrace. Teachers, scholars, the businessmen . . . who spoke in thrilling commands . . . the notion faltered; and suddenly, Howard, who made too much of things, one day discovered that he was becoming old.

He was affrighted, returned to thought, and emerged from the fright with a sort of low joy. Age, at least, meant that you did not have to put up with it much longer. If asked about "it," he would have replied with all certainty that history's greatest gift was that you did not have to take "it" with you.

And then, while walking less than sprightly through a wet autumn in Boston, Howard momentarily stood before the window of a well-groomed, middle-aged and average resturant.

At a table which faced the street, a familiar face chewed, as if the chewer thought of other years and other matters. Brace, that aging Jonah, with his face lined like a walnut, weathered like an old barn, sat in a well-blocked but ancient uniform that bore the worn, dull rings of a lieutenant. Brace stared, half rose from his seat, seemed momentarily joyful. He beckoned.

Howard, with a hot heart and cold feet, entered the resturant.

They spoke at first of predestination, or at least they spoke of vicissitudes. They shook hands, clapped shoulders, ordered wine so expensive that the resturant owner was compelled to hold a long search in the dusty basement he called a cellar. They chortled like mature fools, and about them people sat, watched, smiled with the genuineness of small contempt. In short bursts of conversation men were resurrected, thrust back into the earth—or the sea . . . "Lost overboard up north . . . would of ever thought that a guy from Mississippi would die in ice?"

" . . . dead, of course . . . bad circulation . . . good cook, tho' . . . James the same, just always kind of frail . . . Levere retired, Snow retired—heard he went back to England . . . Conally—charge of a buoy snatcher, Joyce, charge of a snatcher . . . Fallon—engineer on that new west coast icebreaker . . . more'n enough to do on that ship . . . . "

"The rest?"

"I don't know. They come'n go."

"Yourself?"

"It's all different," said Brace. "More money, newer ships, air support." He stared at his wine glass, then looked down at his sleeve. "The world's oldest lieutenant," he said. "Never got off of search and rescue."

"It makes you the last of a kind," said Howard, who, in a vague way, had managed to persuade himself that he had "kept up"—who in a vague way felt that he was asked for endorsement, or asked to accept an apology.

"One of the last. Levere was like that. Chaney. All different now, of course." Brace rubbed at the two dull gold stripes. "It means, at least, that you always have a command."

Wet automobiles passed in the street, and along the sidewalks people moved through a haze that promised winter, a rain so light and dull that it was scarcely even rain. Thick mist, perhaps.

"Married," Brace told Howard. "Nearly fifteen years. The first time didn't take."

"I think . . . another bottle?"

"Can't think of a single reason why not . . . I just remembered. Glass has the deck on a *Morgenthau* class . . . never made the Mafia . . . presume that things kept coming up."

"I certainly remember Glass."

220

Young girls huddled in raincoats, walked beneath umbrellas to protect their hair. A gray-haired woman passed, then two young sailors, then a businessman who strode brisk and grayly. In the streets cars glistened, dull hazed with a sheen of water. Brace and Howard talked, measured—from the lofty view of experience—how much the other drank, matched but did not exceed the amount.

"... had to leave," said Howard. "Figured it all out later. A lot later. When Dane died, I gave out. It was as if I had become unpropped."

Brace, about to light a cigarette, paused. Even before he spoke, before his voice gave other inflections, his face showed that he had dropped the gossipy conversation. He thumbed a lighter. It flared. He lit the smoke, and he slurped smoke with a sort of gratitude for the momentary pause that smoking grants. His thin, narrow nose, below the heavily wrinkled forehead, beside cheeks that were furrowed, running with seams—his nose made him look hawklike. He did not look like Levere had looked, but he looked like a man emigrated from the boundaries of Levere's country, the inshore sea.

"I wanted to be a musician once," said Brace. "Once I was a pretty good musician, for a kid. My father, who was not a musician—" He again drew smoke, this time slowly, and smoke curled around the lines etched above and beneath his eyes—"taught me not to be a musician. Now, I am not exactly certain what that means, but I am willing to talk about Dane."

"We were spooked," said Howard. "Conally and I. I tried to get Dane to take me, instead of you. Maybe I didn't mistrust you. Maybe I just mistrusted everyone but myself."

Brace sipped at his wine, drank deeply, again sipped. Beyond the window a young couple stood in mild argument about the restaurant. They made a decision, walked on.

"The whole crew was spooked," Brace said, "but I'll be double-dog-damn if they weren't good men." He sat, staring through the window into the gray, misting rain. "I've seen strange things since, even stranger than that. The sea sends strange things."

"We thought," said Howard, "that we had received an omen. We believed we understood the omen." He felt in his pocket, found an empty package. Brace pushed his pack of smokes across the table.

"A lot of that crew saw something," Brace said, "but I don't recall that anyone made comparisons. We'll never know if each of those men saw the same thing." He leaned across the table to light Howard's smoke. "I haven't thought about it in a long time," said Brace, "but I *did* think about it for a long time. Years ago—"

"Dane didn't trust me," said Howard. "I don't know how he knew that I was a short timer."

"—and I thought until I got it figured out," said Brace. "Dane was not a complicated man. He was trying to teach me something."

"I don't understand."

"I thought he was trying to kill me," said Brace. "Either that, or I thought we were in some kind of battle." He touched his worn sleeve. "I was afraid to go with him."

"Now I really don't understand."

"Why should you?" Brace said. "I was young and making wrong guesses. Something was going on that you didn't know about."

"You thought he was not a simple man?"

"I hit him" said Brace. "When I was trapped belowdecks on that yacht. I was a kid. I was so scared. I had one foot propped on something that kept trying to roll away, and the water was on my neck. I can still feel it. I had nothing to lose."

"Glass never said . . . no one ever said anything about that."

"I asked them not to," said Brace. "Dane smacked me. I had nothing to lose. I smacked him back. Twice. I laid it on. I bruised everything on that ox except his appetite."

222

Two nuns walked past the restaurant, women, who, if not vowed to silence, knew at least some of the great meanings of silence.

"Snow and Dane were both down there," said Brace. "I learned one thing, but I learned both sides of it."

The world's oldest lieutenant sat beside a man who had so far done but yeoman service in the cause of history. One man dangled the yarns of a life spent saving occasional sparks from the quenching sea, the other mulled catastrophes which had severed the lives of millions. Strangely, perhaps, and perhaps for only a moment, they understood the grand cynicism that ruled them; the knowledge that in this world's hopes and dreams and illusions, in its facades and romantic encumbrances, in the seeming pleasures and devotions of easy belief, of national feeling culled from gutters by their betters, of gods most hopelessly cracked, most disgraced and hopelessly cracked, there are few seas.

"You'll remember," Brace said after a long pause, "how Lamp used to talk. He was always this and that, never before, never behind, just mostly between." He brushed at a worn sleeve that carried its worn and tarnished insignia. The small Coast Guard shield was like a golden, unblinking eye.

"I knew him better," said Howard.

"It is a zoo," said Brace, "but we were wrong about Jonah. And Lamp, so was he. We only had one ghost."

"I wonder if I understand."

"Why should you?" said Brace. "You didn't have one." His face momentarily held a touch of young, potato-peeling wisdom, mast-painting wisdom.

"What didn't I have?"

Brace's face changed, the furrows deepening, and he seemed to own the wisdom of Reeser Lamp, or Levere. He looked into the darkening gray street where automobile headlights were now beginning to glow as if attempting to burn through the mist. "Our fathers," Brace said. "No matter what shape it took, we have only ever had that one ghost. I thought and thought about this."

And Howard, a son only of history, understood with a glad and rushing, sudden opening that there was at least one small history which contained no madness; as Snow had insisted, and which only he, Howard, could tell. Howard asked himself a question, and answered the question while he was asking. When God fails what does Jonah do? Howard finished his drink. He shook hands, made vague promise to meet. He drew on his coat, he backwardly waved, and left.